The Marketing of
Sister B

The Marketing of Sister B

Linda Hoffman Kimball

SIGNATURE BOOKS

SALT LAKE CITY

Cover design by Ron Stucki

The Marketing of Sister B was printed on acid-free paper and was composed, printed and bound in the United States of America.

06   05   04   03   02   6   5   4   3   2   1

Library of Congress Cataloging-in-Publication Data

Kimball, Linda Hoffman.
      The Marketing of Sister B / by Linda Hoffman Kimball.
                  p.   cm.
      ISBN 1-56085-163-5 (pbk.)
        1. Relief Society (Church of Jesus Christ of Latter-day Saints)—Fiction.
      2. Mormon women—Fiction. 3. Marketing—Fiction. I. Title.
      PS3561.I4162 M3 2002
      813'.54—dc21
                                          2002036522

1

If Donna Brooks had known the grief it was about to cause her, she would have never gotten out the cinnamon that morning. If she had really understood the jealousies and strained relations she was about to stir up, she would not have reached for her wooden spoon. If she had had any idea that by plugging in her crock pot that day she was throwing herself into an emotional pressure cooker, she would have simply said to the cosmic powers-that-be: *"Are you nuts?? Count me out, honey, 'cause this gal does not want what you're selling!"* But of course, there was no way to anticipate that favors for a visiting teaching luncheon would turn her into a national celebrity.

Donna Ray Brooks, the forty-three-year-old mother of four and resident of Rottingham, Massachusetts, member of the Commonwealth Falls First Ward, just wanted to make a little something nice for the women in her ward. She was "between callings" at the moment, which suited her fine. She had been released as Primary president and was enjoying a breather. Hank, her husband, had been tapped as the newest member of the high council, so the family had plenty of fingers in the church service pie.

She had loved being the Primary president. In fact, she thrived on coordinating doodads for children: visual aides, the flannel board stories, stickers, word searches, and gospel-oriented goodie bags. But now she was glad that she could shower her creative efforts on anyone she chose, not just on the little lambkins of her prior stewardship.

In the two months since her release, she had tackled the elementary school's newly organized bulletin board for PTA and community notices, she had seen to it that her son's soccer team feasted on cupcakes decorated with geodesic patterns in the frosting, and she had organized the baby shower for Hank's coworker that had proceeded flawlessly from cucumber soup to nut cups.

She decided she liked one-shot deals over long-time obligations. She would sign up to bring all the refreshments to a fifth-grade class party, but she did not want to be the room mother. That's how she worked best. It was not an issue of committing time because she spent enormous amounts of time doing one project after another. It was the psychic obligation of a long haul that bothered her. So it was one morning in September when she called the Relief Society president.

"Hi," she said. "This is Donna Brooks. I remember we have a visiting teaching luncheon next week and I thought I'd volunteer if you have any last minute needs."

"Great!" said Jane Schmidt enthusiastically. "Let me check it out with my counselors and get back to you." About half an hour later, Donna got a call from the homemaking counselor, Claudia Christiansen.

"Oh, Sister Brooks, I'm so delighted that you'll help. It's just so wonderful of you to volunteer like this. I tell you, it's like pulling teeth sometimes. But you just up and volunteer. Why, that's great. Sure wish we could bottle you. Just pop off the cork once in a while when we need a whiff of the real stuff, and there you'd be, Donna Brooks, right under our noses.

"Well, I've carried on here," Claudia continued. "Let me tell you what we could use. We want to have some little favor at each place setting. Something each sister could take home with her, you know, that might remind her of the day. Something maybe a little fun. Maybe cute. It wouldn't have to be super spiritual or anything. Just a little nice thing that would say, 'Sure think you're swell.' In fact, that would make a cute saying on a sponge. Do you know what I mean? When they used the sponge, it would get all puffy and swell up and they'd see the saying, 'Sure think you're swell.' I just thought of that right here on the spot. Oh, you don't have to use that idea. Use your own imagination. I've seen what

2

you did with those Primary tots, so I know you've got a million great ideas.

"We also need somebody to clean up afterwards," she offered, "but I'd rather see you put your talents to better use. I'd say we need about fifty favors. That's optimistic, of course, since we usually don't get that great a turn-out. But this time we're having food and that always draws a crowd. It seems like the kind of thing the sisters might like to invite their visiting teaching folks to even if they haven't seen them for a while, so that will hike up the numbers. Fifty ought to do it."

Claudia was not yet done. "The budget's basically shot," she said, "so it can't be anything too pricey. But I know how you can pull rabbits out of thin air. Just, thank you, thank you for being so willing to do this. I think you're a fabulous person—very special to all of us in the presidency."

Donna hung up aware that her only contribution to the conversation had been to say hello. That was fine. She was pleased that they had challenged her creative abilities. Now, what could she put together that would not cost too much, that would not take too much time, and that would not be something that had been done to death? No grapevine wreaths wrapped with ribbons and dried flowers. No little straw, broad-brimmed hats with dried flowers. She didn't want to work with dried flowers in any configuration.

She toyed with beanbag dolls with round, wooden heads covered with fluffy hair. But she vetoed that for two reasons. First, it would be labor intensive. Second, the finished product would look like the bishop's wife—frizzy haired, round faced, and broad of beam. Thumbs down on magnets, too, even though there were imaginative things that could be done with salt dough, painted-wood slogans, ceramic casts, and little picture frames. But everybody did magnets. Besides, she already had a zillion magnets on her refrigerator.

She would not venture a bookmark again. During President

Kimball's era, she asked one of the Young Women who had bragged about her calligraphy skills to letter the encouraging motto "Do It" on the ribbons. Only after the bookmarks had been distributed to stake dignitaries did she notice that the motto had become "DOLT."

This should be something truly creative. Something no one had ever done before. Something that she could make with things she had around the house. And she wanted the message of the trinket to symbolize the warmth and homey love and enthusiasm she felt for her sisters. She wanted it to be something that they might think about or carry with them in their minds or hearts. Something that might linger awhile and not be tossed into the next trash can, that would bridge the gaps of culture, age, education, and political persuasion in the ward.

That's when she remembered something Sister Christiansen had said. She had mentioned something about bottling, popping the cork, and taking a whiff. That's it! That's what she would do! A big vat of some kind of fragrance that she could pour into those little vials left over from the 4th of July boutonnieres she made for the Veterans of Foreign Wars. She would find little corks, tie some classy ribbon around the neck of the vials, and voila! *Eau d'sisterhood!* When they put a drop on their wrist or behind their ear, they would be surrounded by sisterly affection. Fragrance never fails!

But what should the fragrance be? Nothing too floral. She didn't want a traditional perfume smell. There was too much competition from those vaguely obscene Calvin Klein scents. It should be something fun and down-home like the smell of sawdust. No, that might make a good aftershave, but it wouldn't be right for a visiting teaching luncheon. What were the other evocative smells of the home? A fire in the fireplace. Nice, but too woodsy. She liked the smell of clean kitchen floors and the smell of the dishwasher when it was running because they represented order after chaos. But these were pine and lemon smells and nothing unique about them.

Then the idea came to her. The stroke of heaven-sent genius that sent her into four months of hell. The smell of baking cinnamon buns! This was perfect. The smell of love. The smell of something fabulous in process. It meant comfort and nourishment and nurture. What a perfect combination! Tender, homey, and a little zing of spice. This was it!

To the average homemaker, making perfume would have seemed preposterous. But Donna had a double major in family science and chemistry from BYU. She knew her way around a still, a Bunsen burner, and a crock pot.

In fact, she *did* reach for her crock pot, along with some cheese cloth and a wooden spoon. Then she began gathering sundry ingredients and equipment from the pantry, garage, basement. She got a note pad, as a good scientist would, and recorded her procedure. She put on a Bonnie Raitt tape since she wanted to be loose and funky and energetic. She was cookin'!

By the time the kids were due home from school, the kitchen looked like Betty Crocker, Jonas Salk, and Coco Chanel labs all rolled into one. To make sure her fragrance matched the real thing, she would have to make real cinnamon buns, and that would be perfect for snack time—one of the perks of research and development. Before long, the top of the dryer in the laundry room held fifty-five upright, tiny vials, all lined up in a rack and filled three-quarters full of a handsome auburn fluid. Each vial sported mauve and forest-green ribbons around its neck and a slim cinnamon stick in the ribbons' square knots. Donna could not have scripted a better scene than the one the kids encountered when they walked into the house.

"Wow, Mom! This place smells fantastic!"

"Gee, how many can I have?"

"I could eat the whole house, it smells so good!"

"This is a balm to my troubled soul, Mother mine," said her fourteen-year-old daughter in her dramatic flair.

They consumed one cinnamon bun each, then Donna marched them into the laundry so she could show off her day's non-edible product. The kids were used to this kind of routine. With all the projects she did, they were used to being queried for their input and assessment. Usually they were harsh critics. She'd go back to the drawing board only if there were major, truly persuasive complaints from all four. This time, she probably wouldn't start over. She was exhausted and, after all, this was just a little gewgaw for the sisters, not the cure for cancer.

"These are favors for the visiting teaching luncheon next week," she explained. "It's perfume. Tell me what you think of it. Tell me what feelings come to mind. Tell me if you think the ribbons and cinnamon sticks look okay."

She extracted the cork from one of the vials and passed it briefly under their noses and then had them dab a little on their wrists. They waved their arms around and sniffed, and then their eyes widened and their jaws dropped. After a few moments of reverent silence, the chorus began again.

"Mom, you've outdone yourself!"

"Yummy smells in such a teeny tiny bottle. Mommy, it's my favorite thing you ever made."

"Cool. This is just so cool!"

"Subtle, but it says hearth and home, doesn't it?" again from the fourteen-year-old.

In retrospect, this was a momentous occasion. But in the living of it, it was just another day with the usual chores and routines of being a mother. By the time Hank got home from work, there were plenty of smells to compete with the cinnamon bun aroma from the fabric softener, a Magic Marker for a seventh-grade school project, and the dinner's stir fry. At bedtime, Donna's pride in her visiting teaching favors was supplanted by thoughts

6

of seminary car pooling and the plot line of her Anne Perry mystery.

Getting ready for bed while Hank brushed his teeth, Donna remembered the towels that were still in the dryer. She trooped down, emptied the towels into the laundry basket, and turned to march back upstairs to fold them while they watched TV. But then she put the basket down and took the cork off one of the little vials the kids had sampled and dabbed a little behind her ears. Basket in both hands, she continued upstairs.

Hank was already nestled under the covers chuckling at David Letterman's monologue, clutching the remote, when Donna dumped the towels onto her side of the bed and began to fold them.

"Did you just wash your hair or something?" Hank asked.

"No. It's dry. See?" Donna laughed, tossing her brunette locks with a mock vampiness.

"Something smells terrific. Is it the laundry?"

"Check it out," Donna threw a towel at him; it covered his head. She could hear him sniffing underneath the towel.

"No, no. This isn't it. What is that, that ... tantalizing smell?"

This was unusual. Hank rarely talked during the monologue. Here he was sniffing, rifling through the laundry, stammering with an intriguing growl. Now his arms were around her. He was nuzzling her neck—something that *never* happened during Letterman.

"It's you, Donna! You smell so fabulous!" He tossed the remote on the floor.

Next morning, Donna called Sister Christiansen and told her the favors were ready and that she thought the sisters would be pleased. She said she had made something for the women that was wholesome and heartwarming and that seemed, from all indications, to have just the right amount of spice.

2

The luncheon program went off rather well as these things go. The attendance was better than Sister Christiansen had feared; Donna guessed about forty-five people, including at least five whom she was sure she had never seen before. President Schmidt spoke about the importance of the individual. Donna liked President Schmidt's talks because she always cut to the chase. No flowery anecdotes or worn-out cliches, no admonitions to crank up the statistics. Just clear thoughts presented straight from the hip. Margo Cabot, Donna's best friend in the ward, always complained that President Schmidt lacked "panache." Donna was confused, thinking this had something to do with caramelized candy; but when Margo explained, they both had a good laugh over it.

What President Schmidt lacked in presentation, she made up for in candor. Today she said: "Our ward has a lot of oddballs in it, and some of you are not going to want to visit the women you're assigned to. I know that. But I still want you to visit them. So does Heavenly Father." Somehow you had the feeling that if anyone knew what God wanted, it was President Schmidt. She also announced that the visiting teaching routes had been changed and that new assignments would be distributed Sunday.

There were audible groans when Sister Schmidt announced this. There are few things that shake up a ward like restructuring the visiting teaching routes. Even Donna thought the president could have lowered the boom a little more gently on this topic. Not that it affected Donna much. She had a pleasant enough visiting teaching companion—Gladys Brockbank—and only three women to visit. One of them, a long-time less than active sister, was a surly curmudgeon, so if Donna's assignment changed in some way, it would not be the end of the world.

Beyond that little surprise, the program moved smoothly into a piano and flute duet by Verna Crumrine and her ten-year-old daughter Felicity. Then Ingrid Herlihy, the bishop's hefty better half, spoke about three favorite visiting teaching experiences.

Sister Herlihy was a pleasure to listen to because of her Norwegian accent. She told about going with her visiting teaching sisters for a picnic on the hill where the temple was going to be built. One sister got poison ivy, but that in itself was an inspirational story, the way it cleared up. The second tale was about consistency. She developed a habit of giving her Pekinese dog a heartworm pill on the thirtieth of the month. Since her visiting teachers were always there on the thirtieth, this reminded her to do it, and she was sure that it prolonged Delilah's life. The third story was about the importance of prayer. She said she once had to visit a lady with really pungent body odor. She tried to think of a way to endure the visits and made it a matter of prayer. The next time she visited, she noticed that the woman's kitchen was full of garlic that she consumed for her health. Sister Herlihy went out and bought some compressed garlic tablets for the woman and the odor was never a problem again.

Following Sister Herlihy, Laura Mandarini sang, "Oh, That I Were an Angel," which is always a crowd pleaser. Spiritually massaged, the sisters then left the chapel and proceeded into the cultural hall. The chicken and broccoli casseroles steamed on the buffet tables. Rose-colored tablecloths adorned the tables set with plastic plates and utensils. Each table had a pitcher of water with lemon wedges, salt and pepper shakers, a stick of butter, and a wicker basket with rolls. Donna spied her dainty vials at each setting looking absolutely perfect on the rose table cloths.

"Sisters, if you would just pause for a moment," began Sister Christiansen, slapping the squealing microphone. "We have a few announcements. Take a seat wherever you find an empty space. No name cards. You know, sisters, we thought about that, but it's too formal, even though we wouldn't want to forget even one sister after what President Schmidt said about the importance of the individual. No, no, no. Introduce yourselves to everyone at your table. We'd like you to try a little game and ask each other what animal you would be if you could pick. That way you can get a feel of each other's spirit on a more personal level. I believe we have some non-members here among us, and we especially want to welcome you and make you feel at home. So, please sisters, yes, just come right along and take your seats for a moment. You'll see we've got your plates at the table, and—when the time comes, not quite yet, mind you—take your plates to the serving table in two lines.

"First, though, we have some thank you's to make. Sister Schmidt for organizing our lovely music and program this morning (gentle applause). Second, for the food, thanks goes to, well, you know, Heavenly Father, which Sister Martha Duncan will say when she offers our blessing. But besides Him, the 'hands that prepared it' part, just keep in mind that those hands belong to Sisters Jennifer Blocker, Rosamund Thatcher, and Francis Kelly. Thank you so much (more gentle applause). Then to me for heading up the decorations, which of course wasn't all my doing. Heavens no! Sisters Karen Beesley, Doreen Putnam, and Sarah Miles set and decorated our tables. And the oh-so-lovely bottles at your tables are courtesy of Sister Donna Brooks who made each of us a perfumed oil so we can carry the feeling of our meeting with us in our hearts after we leave. I suppose you could put it right on your hearts, if you wanted to dab a little there. But do that part at home. I'd personally put it on the pulse points like Sister Butler taught us about in Homemaking last year. Do you remember that, ladies? Such a fine lesson. Anyway, thanks to all of you who made this afternoon possible, from the bottom of my heart, which is where I'll carry the feeling of this meeting with me all week long and into my daily life and for all eternity."

At this point, Martha Duncan hustled up to the microphone. She snatched it from Sister Christiansen so she could say the blessing before the steam stopped rising from the casseroles.

When Donna returned to her table with her food, her luncheon table partners were Margo, Elizabeth Potter, Juliet Benton, Doreen Putnam, and a woman whom Donna didn't know, who apparently came with Doreen. The woman looked different from the rest of the ladies there. Snazzier. Better groomed, or it may have been her outfit. Most of the other women seemed to be dressed for church. No, they seemed dressed *like* church—plain and frugal with few accoutrements, everything durable and staid. This woman had what even Donna could recognize as panache. Her make-up was perfect. She had a smart suit, a crisp cotton shirt that must have been a bear to iron, and jewelry that caught your eye but didn't overwhelm.

"Hello, hello," said Margo, extending her hand to the new woman. "I just love your earrings. I was eying them during the meeting. I'm Margo Cabot. Are you visiting with Doreen today?"

"Hello, Margo. I'm Lucy Hobbes from New York City." Lucy nodded and smiled to Donna and to the other women at the table.

"Lucy and I were roommates at Columbia. She's made it big out there," Doreen said.

"What brings you here today?" said Margo.

"I haven't seen Doreen and Matt since they got married a year ago. I thought it was about time to catch up," Lucy said.

"What do you do?" Donna asked.

That was a question Donna herself hated. When she attended office functions with Hank and people asked her what she did, she never knew how to answer the question. What would be appropriate? I manage a small collection of bipedal primates? I am a chauffeur? A diplomat? She usually mumbled something about being a community volunteer and that sufficed.

"I'm in marketing," Lucy said.

"Would that be Star Market, dear?" asked Elizabeth Potter. Elizabeth was nearly eighty and had hearing problems. Donna noticed Margo's eyes roll.

11

"It isn't that kind of marketing," Margo said, raising her voice a bit and speaking slowly and distinctly.

"What aspect of marketing *are* you involved in?" Margo asked. Margo was normally energetic, but she seemed even more enlivened now.

"I watch for new products and connect them with agents, promoters. If my intuition is good, we all skip merrily to the bank," she explained with a chuckle.

"I do my shopping at Star Market and they have bank machines now right next to the check-out counter. It's very convenient," said Elizabeth. "You should try it."

"Sounds like a good idea," said Lucy graciously. "How about you ladies? Who are you? How do you fill your time?"

There was a moment of silence at the table. This, Donna assumed, was the time required for the mental gymnastics demanded by the question. Margo leaped out with hearty introductions. No one needed to make up games about what kind of animal they would like to be when Margo could cover that in a bullet point or two, all neatly packaged. Donna smiled

"The matriarch among us," Margo began as she took hold of Elizabeth's two frail shoulders, "is Elizabeth Potter. Mother of eight, grandmother and great-grandmother, and an extraordinary quilter. She has practically memorized all the scriptures, including some of the more lurid passages of the Old Testament, and she can tell you her genealogy back to four separate royal lines. She has also experimented with sericulture just like in the nineteenth-century."

"What's sericulture?" asked Elizabeth.

"You know, when you try to raise silk worms in your basement."

"Oh, yeah. I guess I've settled for vermiculture under the kitchen sink."

"Here's Juliet," Margo continued undaunted. "What's your last name, Juliet?"

"I'm Juliet Benton," she said quietly. She seemed ready to speak for herself, but Margo carried on.

"Why, you and Juliet have something in common. Juliet just moved here from New York City, didn't you?"

"I moved from Ithaca, not Manhattan. It's nice to meet you."

"Anyway, there is a common ground there, I'm sure. Juliet's our ward scholar. If you want to know anything about German history, just call her."

"Actually, it's art history," Juliet corrected.

"I'm sorry, Juliet," said Margo. "Art? Don't let anybody know that or they'll nab you for the visual aids!"

"I don't *do* art, I teach it. The painters, the periods, the influences," she said.

"I still think they'll nab you," Margo cautioned. "Next we have Doreen whom you know, and I'm Margo Cabot. I work in the dental offices of Drs. Abbott and Costelli. Is that hilarious? I can't tell you how often we hear patients comment about that. Anyway. I've got two daughters off at college. One at the Y and one at Amherst. I'm a transplanted Idahoan, and I freed myself from the world's worst husband ten years ago. I'm a frustrated capitalist and I want your life!"

Everyone laughed, but it was true, Donna knew.

"And last but not least, we have Donna Brooks. Donna is smart as a whip, double major in college. She has four lovely children and a husband who is a bit of a hunk, if she doesn't mind me saying so. Donna is really creative. Why, these jars here at the table are her brainchild." Margo held up one of the little bottles of oil.

"Just what is this, Donna?" Lucy asked. "It looks so lovely."

"I thought they were for consecrated oil," Margo whispered to Donna out the corner of her mouth.

"I haven't quite thought of the right name for it, but it's like an essential oil. I wanted a fragrance that brings to mind home and hearth," she said, remembering her daughter's alliterative de-

13

scription. "I'm quite fond of it. It smells great, and everyone at home is pleased with it. Take out the corks and dab a little on. You don't need to get anywhere near your hearts."

The five women gamely uncorked their vials and sampled the oil. Once again the reaction was euphorically positive. The ladies at the neighboring table became aware of the subtle fragrance and soon everyone in the room was dabbing on their cinnamon scented oil.

Suddenly Elizabeth Potter stood up and began reciting verses from the Bible in a louder voice than anyone had ever heard from her:

> And cinnamon, and odors, and ointments, and frankincense, and wine, and oil, and fine flour, and wheat, and beasts, and sheep, and horses, and chariots, and slaves, and the souls of men. For who can find a virtuous woman? Her price is far above rubies. The heart of her husband doth safely trust in her, so that he shall have no need of spoil. She girdeth her loins with strength and strengtheneth her arms. Strength and honor are her clothing; and she shall rejoice in the time to come. Give her of the fruit of her hands, and let her own works praise her in the gates!

Lucy Hobbes leaned over to Donna, handed her a business card, and whispered, "Could you give me your phone number? We've got to talk business."

3

After Elizabeth's rousing proclamation, Donna felt conspicuous. She was used to good-natured accolades, but there was a vigor in the reaction to her perfume that she found unnerving. People swarmed over to her, buzzing with questions and compliments. Thank heaven the desserts appeared and everyone migrated to the "Make Your Own Sundae" table.

As she built her own dish of neapolitan with chocolate sauce, Donna wondered what Lucy meant by talking "business." She didn't have an opportunity to talk to her privately. When the kudos cooled, Doreen and Lucy had already left.

At home, life was back to its typical domestic whirlwind. Twelve-year-old Simon was playing Stratego in the family room with a buddy. Pizza crusts and empty pop cans cluttered the kitchen counter. Simon had a big smear of tomato sauce on his cheek. He was too lost in stratagems to worry about so mundane a detail. Donna tore a paper towel off the roll, dampened it, and swiped the goo off Simon's face.

"Mommmm, stop!" he whined.

Fourteen-year-old Stephanie was stretching the phone cord from the kitchen down the basement stairwell, giggling. She was talking to her friend Roxanne. Normally she didn't giggle. For Stephanie, life was too serious, too catastrophic, or much too urgent for giggles. But something about Roxanne brought out Stephanie's lighter side. Roxanne, a bubble-headed, boy-crazy gum chewer and the least likely cohort Donna could have imagined for her daughter, was a therapeutic gift from God.

Donna heard the garage door open and looked out to see Hank and the two youngest boys pulling into the driveway. She went out to greet them. Hank had taken Ben, seven years old, and Nate, ten, swimming while she was at the luncheon. The boys dashed out of the car and tossed wet trunks and towels into a jumble on the mudroom floor.

"How'd it go?" asked Hank, giving her a peck on the cheek.

"Just fine," Donna said. "I think the oil was a hit."

"Yeah, I bet," chuckled Hank. "I wonder if you'll get updates tomorrow from the elders quorum on what *they* think."

"Doreen had a friend there who was some kind of executive

from Manhattan. The woman gave me her card and said she wanted to talk business."

"What kind of business?"

"About the cinnamon oil, I guess."

"Really? Are you sure she didn't want you in her calling circle for investments?" Hank laughed.

"I hadn't thought of that. Do you think? I thought she wanted to talk to me about the oil, but I could be wrong. Oh, I doubt I'll hear from her anyway. Too bad. She seemed really nice. Very chic, actually. She was Doreen's roommate at Columbia. She's not Mormon, I don't think. But for a few minutes, I had this fantasy that she was going to make me rich and famous. Wouldn't that be nice? We could get a maid. We could hire a cook."

"If you were rich and famous, you could hire me as the cook," Hank laughed. He loved cooking, especially ethnic cuisine—Szechuan beef and pea pods that made your mouth drool and spicy fajitas, that kind of thing. Donna would be glad to turn her droning daily ritual over to Hank, but practicality dictated otherwise. She was the one who scrambled at 5:30 every evening to answer the all-important, "What's for supper?"

When Stephanie emerged from the stairwell, a red welt on her face where the phone had been pressed, she said: "Roxanne and I are going to the mall this afternoon. Can you take us in a half hour?"

"I suppose so. What's at the mall?" This was a question a mother didn't need to ask. She knew what happened at the mall. Socialization of the species. The preening dance of the wild happened at the mall. Clearance sales on bed linens drew the matriarchs, but for adolescents there was much more at stake: the pecking order, plumage, pride and prejudice—all in front of Payless Shoe Source.

But Stephanie wasn't a mall kind of gal. She was a library gal and a theatrical stage gal and the type you'd find lying prostrate on the living room floor with earphones blasting not Britney but Wagner's *The Ring of the Niebelungen*. So what *was* up at the mall?

"Roxanne's mom thinks this is just a mall cruising, but Roxanne's going to get her a birthday present. Her mom's turning forty and there's a surprise party tonight. I said I'd help her find something that her mother needs instead of something frivolous—the kinds of things I'd get for you like pantyhose that hides veins or an Abs Roller or something."

Hank laughed. Donna groaned. She tried to think of the lather of kind comments she had received from the Relief Society luncheon.

"That's a sweet family thing—a surprise party," Donna tried to accentuate the positive, ignore the negative, and not mess with Mr. In-Between, as she recalled the apostolic counsel.

"Well yes, the family is hosting it, but it's for a lot of the Wheelers' friends and neighbors. Roxanne invited me. I guess they don't know you guys well enough. Maybe they think you wouldn't be particularly valuable contributors to the party."

Another groan.

Just then the phone rang and Stephanie grabbed it before the second ring. "It's for you, Mom. Lucy Hobbes." She handed her the phone as she headed upstairs to get ready.

"Lucy?"

"Hi, Donna. I'm glad I caught you. I was so taken by the perfume you made for the ladies' luncheon. I think it's sellable if you have interest in seeing it marketed. I just talked to a promoter at Big Apple, my company, and as it turns out, she's going to be in Boston tonight and wants to meet you. Is that possible? She'll probably bat some ideas around. Of course, I can't guarantee she'll be interested, but I'm optimistic. Are you available for dinner at, say, seven? Your husband, too, if he's free."

"Why, yes, yes. That sounds wonderful," stammered Donna.

"Great. How does Legal Seafood sound? I'll reserve a table if that's okay. The one at Kendall Square. Oh, bring a recent photo and a sample of the product. We'll see you tonight, then?"

"Sure."

Donna hung up the phone. She threw her arms around Hank and gave him a big kiss. "Put on your lobster bib, honey! We're going out! The woman from New York is interested in the perfume and she's invited us out to meet a promoter!"

"I didn't think you were serious," said Hank.

"O ye of little faith," laughed Donna. "Oh, dear me. I don't have a recent photograph except for the ones from New Hampshire last August. I'm sure a shot of me in a Brooks Family Reunion t-shirt is not what they're looking for."

"Don't they have those 'four shots for a dollar' booths at the mall? Maybe you could go with Stephanie," suggested Hank.

"What? My mother's going with me to the mall?" gasped Stephanie who had just galloped down the front stairs. "Are you kidding?"

"Your mother and I are going to go out with an agent tonight who may want to market the cinnamon oil," said Hank, his nose in the air.

"Seriously!?" Stephanie shrieked. "Someone's interested in your cinnamon essence? I love that stuff, Mom. I absolutely love it, and I think this is utterly terrific. Somebody from New York? How impressive! But what does this have to do with going to the mall?"

"I need a photograph. I don't know, but I also think this might be a good excuse to find a new outfit. What do you think? Something for the 'dress for success' crowd? Hank, maybe you could take some pictures of me and we could take the roll to one of those one-hour finishing places."

"Mom, I know what to do! Let's take you to Glamour Shots! Cool!" Stephanie squealed. The high pitch, the shrillness that was foreign to Stephanie, brought the boys clambering into the kitchen.

"What's wrong?" Ben and Nate asked in union.

"Did someone get hurt?" Simon asked anxiously.

"That sounded like when Mr. Kemper ran over a squirrel!" Simon's friend Aaron said.

"Everything's just fine. Remember this moment, though," said Hank, putting his arm around Donna's shoulder. He kissed her. Then turning to the kids, he said: "This woman who stands among pizza crusts and swimsuits will soon be famous. She will soon no longer be just your mom, she will be Everymom. She will no longer be the maker of doodads but the maker of millions. All of America will look to her ..."

"Yeah, yeah, right, Dad," Simon groaned as he and Aaron trudged back to watch *The Princess Bride*. "Just give me a bigger allowance," he said.

Hank shrugged, gave Donna another kiss, and then followed Nate and Ben downstairs.

"You really do need a make-over, Mom," Stephanie said, snapping a gray hair from the side of her head. "If you're meeting with an agent, you simply *can't* go like you are."

"Well, thank you so much, dear," said Donna sarcastically. "It's hard sweeping cinders from the fireplace all day long and no fairy godmother. Whatever will I do?"

"I know, I know," groaned Stephanie, not really catching the sarcasm. "But wouldn't that just be the best solution? Come along with Roxanne and me, and I'll do whatever it takes to get you up to speed—at least externally. Roxanne's waiting, and if we're really going to fix you, we'd better go now."

Donna went upstairs and caught a glimpse of herself in the mirror. She wasn't such a sorry specimen even if Stephanie thought so. Besides, there is more to a book than its cover. Beauty's only skin deep ... All that glitters is not gold. She had about exhausted her list of cliches when she heard Stephanie honking the horn for her.

19

4

At the mall, Stephanie and Roxanne escorted Donna to Glamour Shots but discovered that the photos wouldn't be ready the same day. Just as well, Donna thought, as she looked at the sample photographs lining the store walls. Everyone looked dewy-eyed and air-brushed. Donna had never worn lipstick until she was thirty-five, and she couldn't see herself looking like that. She'd be just as well off going to Plymouth and having her picture taken in Pilgrim garb with a faux *Mayflower* background.

Since the photo session was out, Roxanne and Stephanie wandered off to Victoria's Secret "looking for something for her mother." Donna headed to Filene's, found a royal blue, smart-looking pants suit on sale and bought it. It looked good on her, not too tight, which was reassuring. She enjoyed the tickle of rebellion purchasing something she wouldn't be able to wear to most church functions. Passing by the accessories, she spied a bright floral scarf with some royal blue highlights and snapped that up too. Oh, shoes. She had four pair: all-purpose walking shoes, black heels, white heels, and some two-toned brown-and-black pumps. What should she get for her new suit? She veered toward the shoe department, but then her conscience got the better of her. Her two-toned shoes would be fine.

She bought a few things she needed for the house—light bulbs, vitamin C, a garden trowel to replace the one that rusted in the yard, and some sport socks for Hank and Simon. Miraculously, Stephanie and Roxanne were ready at the appointed place and time.

"What did you end up getting?" Donna asked as they pulled out of the mall parking lot.

"My mother is hard to buy for, Mrs. Brooks? So Stephanie and me? We went around and bought, like, lots of little things? Stephanie thought we could put them in a basket, and well, it's an awesome idea? So like, we got her a loofa brush and some scented soap? And, um, nail polish in a super shade of purple that is really so cool, I think she'll just love it? And some little heart stickers? And what else, Stephanie? Help me, like, remember; my brain is like gone?" Roxanne broke into a giggle.

"We bought her some pencils with her zodiac sign and horoscope on them. Mrs. Wheeler is into her horoscope, Mom," said Stephanie. "And at the nutrition center, I suggested that we get her a jar of dietary fiber additive like you use, but Roxanne saw a ginseng root balm and a lavender eye pillow, so we got her those things, instead. Oh, and Mom! This is where you can be of assistance. May we give Mrs. Wheeler one of your little bottles of the cinnamon oil? It would be the perfect addition."

"Sure you can. A birthday remembrance from me," Donna said. She was pleased that Stephanie's vocabulary remained generally unscathed despite her contact with Roxanne's teenspeak.

At 6:15 that night, Donna and Hank pulled out of the driveway with everything all squared away. A sitter was tending the younger boys since Simon was spending the night at Aaron's and Stephanie was with Roxanne. The boys had been fed, the dishwasher was running, an acceptable video had been procured and was running. Hank had taken a roll of pictures of Donna in her snazzy clothes and got them developed at the one-hour place. For the first time in her memory, there were actually three decent shots to choose from. Donna let Stephanie cast the deciding vote.

On Donna's lap in the car was a little box. Inside, stuffed all around with tissue, was a vial of Donna's concoction. "You know, Hank," Donna said, "we really should think of a name for this stuff. Got any suggestions?"

"Hmm," he thought. "I'm not very good at this."

"Humor me. Think of it as brainstorming. You know—any idea is okay, no judging or screening. Just a free flow of ideas."

"How about Husband's Delight?"

"No."

"Hey, you said no judging or screening," Hank fussed.

"I lied."

"Well, then, how about Spice Is Nice?" Hank ventured.

"That's not too awful," Donna said. "But something more cinnamony."

"Cinnamon Spice, maybe? How about something plain like that?"

"It needs to say it's an oil or perfume, not a food additive," said Donna. "Something that combines spice and oil."

"Spoil!" Hank laughed.

"Please! But maybe Cinnamonoil or Cinnamoil?" Donna suggested.

"That has a nice ring to it, I think."

"You think so? You don't think it sounds like a cartoon character? You know, Olive Oil's cousin from Hoboken?"

"No, I kind of like it. Cinnamoil. CINNAMOIL," Hank experimented with the pronunciation and proclaimed it in tenor, bass, and falsetto voices.

"Enough, enough!" Donna laughed, as they pulled into the parking lot.

Lucy Hobbes was with an equally stylish woman, presumably the promoter, at the Legal Seafood reception counter. Handshakes all around and pleasant chatter. They sat down and perused the menu. Gloria Hewitt, the promoter, was an effervescent woman who put Donna at ease. Donna managed to lower her expectations about the oil and decided that for now, she would focus on the present reality of a good meal on someone else's dime. Toss in the benefit of attention from total strangers and her mood was cheerful, too.

Seventh Heaven, she thought. Maybe Seventh Heaven would be a good name. She would see what they said when they talked business.

After appetizer chowders and before the entrees arrived, Lucy dove right in. "Donna, I told Gloria about the magnificent scent you created for your ladies' luncheon," she began. "Before you arrived, I showed her my own sample from the party. Of course, I'm not going to part with mine, so I'm glad you brought an extra bottle. This is a remarkable aroma. It's heartwarming and endearing, but ... there's more. Something vital and unforgettable."

"I agree with you there," chuckled Hank.

"Before Lucy steals my thunder, let me just tell you, Donna," Gloria said, "that I think this is truly original and appealing and absolutely marketable. Since Lucy told me about this on the phone, and especially since I've had a chance to see it and smell it myself, I've been doing lots of thinking about how to pitch this gem. It has several strengths. First, it taps into a new but fairly secure market—essential oils or their knock-offs. Folks used to be a little squeamish about oils because they sounded hippie or something, but now everyone has a product line. All the cosmetic companies carry essential oils or relabeled some of their existing products to fill the demand.

"Second, we're coming up on the high production season, which is perfect—I mean, it's the *perfect* time to strike, especially since your oil has a holiday quality—family around the dinner table, carols in the street, cookies in the oven, a romantic fire in the fireplace," Gloria continued.

Hank sighed, squeezing Donna's hand.

"With this oil, someone from the most dysfunctional family would still believe in the Walton family Christmas. From what Lucy said about the church women, females from all the demographic categories should respond to this scent—housewives, the intelligentsia, the elderly, young women, the corporates. I'm thinking of a to-die-for holiday stocking stuffer. That's how I see this. Get the price point low so everyone can afford it, but not so low that it's undervalued. I think there could be huge interest at first, then probably a slow down to a steady volume. Think Cab-

23

bage Patch Kid and Tickle Me Elmo. What do you think? Are you interested in having us market your product?"

Donna looked at Hank. She thought about Stephanie's comment about how bland her life was. Bland, bland, bland! She knew it was true. She thought about Hank and his fajitas. She thought about Simon and his bigger allowance and that even the younger boys were getting older and didn't need her in the same way anymore. Was she game for this kind of venture? Didn't she need something fun? Wouldn't this be just the thing?

"Would you excuse Hank and me for a minute," Donna asked suddenly, pulling Hank up from his seat.

"Sure, sure," Gloria said.

Donna drew Hank out to the corridor by the restrooms and grabbed him by his lapels. "What do you think, Hank? If I say yes, this might mean a lot of change. Not just for me, but for you, for the kids, for the whole family," she whispered.

"I know, I know. But this is so exciting for you. It's exciting for all of us, honey. If you have the stamina for it, I'm behind you. Let's not get carried away, you know. Maybe she's giving you the pie-in-the-sky routine and nothing will happen. Or ..."

"Or it might be exciting!" squealed Donna.

"I think it could be a great adventure for all of us."

"OK, OK, let's pray about it," Donna whispered as someone walked passed on their way to the restroom.

"Sure. Of course."

"I'll say it." Donna bowed her head. "Heavenly Father, if this is the stupidest thing we've ever done, if this is really not what you have in mind for us, stop us now because I really want to do this and I've got to tell you that I'm so excited I could scream. But we'll be quiet for a little bit now, and if this is something bad, let us know."

Donna and Hank kept their heads bowed. Donna's hands still clutched his lapels. An on-looker would have thought this was a very earnest tete-à-tete. After about a minute of silence,

24

Donna opened her eyes, feeling much calmer. Hank looked at her, nuzzled her neck where she applied the oil before they left the house, and gave her a big hug.

"I think we should do it," she said.

"I'm with you all the way."

Donna led as they walked to the table, smiling and holding hands.

"Everything OK?" Lucy asked.

"Everything's fine," Donna said, beaming. "I'll do it. Where do I sign?"

5

The name of Gloria's firm was Big Apple. As it turned out, the company would have papers ready for Donna to sign in New York on Tuesday. She was to fly first-class, no less! When she left Legal Seafood Saturday night, she thought Tuesday couldn't come soon enough.

But time does funny things. Sunday morning, as the family pulled into the ward parking lot, Donna spied Margo.

"Margo, you are never going to believe this!" She rushed over to her, letting Hank go in with the kids to nab their usual bench.

"Let's see, what might I never believe?" laughed Margo. "I might not believe you spent the night in jail. I might not believe I'll lose those last ten pounds. I might never ... "

"Hush, Margo! Let me tell you!" she whispered. "I'm going to sell my perfume! That woman at the visiting teaching lunch, Lucy Hobbes. Hank and I went out to dinner with her last night and with a promoter from her company, and I said yes!"

"You said yes!" squealed Margo. "She said yes!" Margo trumpeted to no one in particular in the parking lot.

"They're going to think you just proposed to me!" laughed Donna.

"I'm so excited!" Margo added, gripping Donna's arm so tightly it left a mark. "So what does this mean, anyway?"

"I go to New York Tuesday to sign contracts and then they do whatever to make me famous!" Donna said.

"Can I drive you down to New York? Can I go with you? I'll get off work. Abbott won't mind. Please?" Margo begged. "Let me live vicariously!"

"They're flying me down. Can you believe it?"

"Oh, darn. Well, I mean, good for you, but I would have liked to come along for the power ride," Margo sighed. Just then, they heard the opening bars of "Called to Serve" booming from the chapel.

"Paul Prendergast must be at the organ again. Everything's fortissimo to him. Let's go in," said Donna. "And Margo, let's let this be our little secret, okay?"

Distracted and rummaging through her scripture case, Margo muttered: "Whatever you say, Donna. Whatever you say."

Later in Relief Society, Donna was tapped to give the opening prayer. As she was about to sit down, Sister Christiansen caught her by the sleeve. "Sisters, can I have your attention for one wee little minute? Thank you. I've kept Sister Brooks here for just a tiny bit as our spotlight sister."

At that moment, Sister Christiansen pressed a remote and a spot light at the back of the room turned on and shone directly at Donna. Donna held her hand to her eyes to keep the glare out. Sister Christiansen slapped a smiling sunshine face made of construction paper to Donna's chest with a thwack. The first thought Donna had was what kind of mark the tape would leave on her blouse. As she was mentally considering laundry remedies for tape on clothing, Sister Christiansen said, "Remember those little bottles of perfume she made for our visiting teaching luncheon?"

This brought a crescendo of contended sighs and murmurs

of assent. "Well, Sister Brooks is heading to New York this week to sell them nationwide! Our own dear Sister Donna Brooks is going to join the ranks of the Osmonds, the Marriotts, our beloved Brother Huntsman, and that seven-habits guy, what's-his-name? Isn't it amazing, here from our very own circle of sisters, our own Donna, whom we all know and love, is gonna be a star! Doesn't this build your testimonies? Won't this be a boon? By such small and simple things are great things brought to pass! And if I do say so myself, I was the one who thought of asking her to make something for us. So thank you, Sister Brooks, for being our spotlight sister of the week."

The spotlight turned off, leaving Donna again blinded. Staggering to her seat, she contemplated the assemblage of sisters. It was as if Moses was parting the Red Sea. On the right was water—all the tender-hearted, emotional sisters who gazed up admiringly and teary-eyed at her. The dry land was on the other side—the more practical souls sat on the left, peering through slitted lids with "I'll believe it when I see it" and "Who does she think she is?" seeping silently from their pores.

When she made it back to her chair, she was sure she was beet red. Margo put her arm around her shoulders and gave her a squeeze. "Pays to have friends to do a little PR for you, doesn't it?"

"I told you to keep quiet, Margo," Donna hissed. She felt faint.

"I guess I missed that part," Margo said dismissively. "Anyway, knowing you, you'd keep your light under that bushel of yours. I think it's my job to help you shine, shine, shine!" She squeezed Donna's shoulder again and then kept her arm over the top of her chair. Possessively, Donna thought. It annoyed her.

On a normal Sunday, she would have disliked being "broken into groups," but Donna was relieved to hear what the teacher had in mind today. She passed out slips of paper with questions about fellowshipping non-members. Donna found herself in a group with Sister Schmidt, Juliet Benton (the art history professor), and some random mother-in-law from St. George visiting a new grandbaby.

"Our question is, 'Name some ways we can expose our non-member friends to the good influences available through church membership,'" Sister Schmidt said flatly.

The mother-in-law spoke up. "I think our youth programs are so valuable in this day and age. It's so nice to see youth doing wholesome things. I would tell my friends about our teenagers. Well, I would if I knew anyone who had teenagers who wasn't already in the ward. That's an opportunity you have here in the mission field."

"I met my first Mormon at a service project," said Juliet.

"See?" said the mother-in-law. "That's how we fellowship people."

"The service project was sponsored by the Catholic Charities at Cornell and one of the teenage runaways who showed up at the soup kitchen was Mormon."

"Oh," said the mother-in-law.

"How did you find out he was Mormon?" asked Sister Schmidt.

"He had one of those really short hair cuts with designs carved in. His design said CTR and I asked him what it stood for," Juliet said.

"Well, there you go," stammered the mother-in-law.

"Any other ideas?" asked Sister Schmidt.

Silence reigned. Donna was about to comment, but the teacher asked them to reassemble their chairs. Donna looked over at Juliet. She didn't know Juliet very well, but her remarks this morning intrigued her. Soup kitchens? Runaways? Catholic Charities? This from that young slip of a thing who hovered around the land of the nerds? Juliet's dark hair was pulled back into an attractive French braid, but the little wire rim glasses practically screamed "intellectual." She dressed well but with nondescript earrings and sensible shoes. She struck Donna as exotic, even as reserved and polite as she was. Maybe it was because she was a convert. You never knew where converts came from, what life had been like living on the shifting moral sands of Babylon.

It must be tough to find a date, Donna thought. Here she is, stuck in a family ward where the only single guys are over sixty. Even in a crowd of younger folks, lots of guys would be scared off by the initials—not the JB but the Ph.D.

The teacher held forth with a cheerleader's pep, asking women to represent their little groups. The mother-in-law sprang up to share their thoughts, although they didn't resemble their brief conversation as Donna recollected it.

Sister Schmidt stood up at the end of the lesson. "Sisters, we have your new routes for visiting teaching. Please take these last few minutes to confer with your partner, if she's here, and get your schedules worked out. Not much left of July, you know. Chop, chop!" She passed out little index cards with names and assignments.

Donna looked at hers. Well, well. Her new companion was Juliet Benton. The people she visited were the same except for one addition—Margo.

6

The phone rang just after lunch. It was Margo. "Why did you rush out after church?" she demanded. "I wanted to hear more about your big news!"

"This big news isn't anything yet, and I wish you hadn't blabbed it to the Relief Society," said Donna.

"Oh, don't be silly. I'm serious that you need a good manager. Besides, I'm jealous," Margo continued.

"There's nothing to be jealous about," Donna said.

"Yes, just you wait!"

"Let's change the subject," Donna said. "What's your schedule like for the end of this week? I'm your new visiting teacher."

"Who's your companion?" Margo asked.

"Juliet Barton."

"She's nice, I guess. A bit of a snore, though, don't you think? It bugged me that she kept correcting me at that luncheon."

"Margo, you mangled all the facts of her life."

"Well, still. I think she's a little snooty," said Margo. "But pick a day *after* you've been to New York so you can tell me about it! Every juicy detail!"

That was just the first call of the afternoon. A dozen more followed. Eight were from well wishers from the Relief Society, some of whose names Donna didn't recognize. They were probably serving in an auxiliary. It's hard to put names to faces with those folks.

Then the elders quorum president and the high priest group leader called asking for a bulk buy of the oil for their wives for upcoming anniversaries.

"Sure. Sure," said Donna. She was flattered.

Then the Stake Relief Society president called asking if Donna would plan ahead and make some of the little bottles for next March's stake Relief Society birthday bash.

"I'd be delighted to!" said Donna, beaming with pride.

Then the new stake Public Affairs director, Sister Monson, called. "Sister Brooks," she began. Her voice was so delicious and dreamy—a cross between a lullaby and the salutation of Gabriel. "It has come to my attention that you've been given a lucrative offer to market your party favor nationwide. Congratulations! And may I add, I've had the opportunity to sample your product, and my, it is celestial! I'm sure you'll enjoy success with this!"

"Um, I haven't been offered anything lucrative," stammered

Donna. "I'm just going down to New York to sign some papers. I don't know what the figures will be."

"Oh, I see. The church rumor mill got a little ahead of itself again," chuckled Sister Monson. "But not to worry. I still have confidence in the excellence of your product, and that's why I'm calling."

Donna didn't really care why Sister Monson was calling. She loved to listen to her voice. She could be describing sheep bloat and Donna would listen with rapt attention. But of course, this cooing confidence was nice, too!

"As I say, I would like to provide assistance for you, should this product take off as I expect it may. I have some contacts in the business world. I know a good lawyer, and I believe, given the proper grooming, this could be a blessing for you and your family and for the church. Promoting the image of the church is important. You have a splendid talent, Sister Brooks. Don't bury it in the ground like the unwise servant. Let me help you magnify it in whatever ways I can."

There was something less charming about being warned about being an unwise servant, but overall, Donna was still ecstatic. "Yes, yes, of course," she said.

"Will you give me a call when you return from New York and fill me in on your meeting?" asked Sister Monson.

"Yes, yes, of course," Donna said again. She scribbled down the phone number.

As Donna snuggled under her covers that night, she tried to explain to Hank the content of the conversation. She realized she wasn't quite sure what she had agreed to. "I guess she just offered to help," said Donna.

"Help what?" asked Hank.

"She said something about 'promoting the image of the church' and about 'proper grooming,'" Donna said.

"Between her grooming and Stephanie's make-over, I wonder if we'll even recognize you," Hank mused.

"Don't be silly," Donna said. "I think this lady was just wishing me well and offering me assistance generally if something should come up. I told her I'd call when I get back from New York."

Monday morning, Donna met the typical mayhem of school lunches, missing shoes, scattered backpacks, and breakfast spills, but with more aplomb than usual. "Remember, tomorrow after I send you off to school, I'm heading to New York for the day," Donna said. She expected a few oohs and ahhhs.

"Whatever," said Stephanie. That seemed to sum up the kids' feelings all the way around.

After the children were launched, the phone started ringing again. More Relief Society well wishers, a telemarketer with a vinyl siding company, a reminder from the dentist for Hank's appointment. Then Mrs. Wheeler, Roxanne's mother, called.

"Donna, I wanted to let you know how much I loved—L-O-V-E-D—the scent you included in my birthday basket. There's something about it. I put some on before bed and Randy suddenly lived up to his name! At the party, you'd think everyone was stoned! Are you sure that stuff is legal? Wow! So, where can I get some more? I want to send some to my sister in Omaha. What's it called? I didn't see a label."

"I'm just talking to someone about marketing it," Donna began. She explained a little about how it came to be.

"You *made* that stuff? Have you been hiding a still in your basement? It's intoxicating, Donna. Don't take this wrong, but I would not have figured you for such a, well—how can I say this?—an interesting person. I mean, there you are every day— church lady, doing PTA, driving around like a little Hausfrau, and I mean that in the best sense of the word—and whoa! Here you are whipping up this heavenly goo right in our neighborhood! Say, Donna, do you want me to read your chart for you? I can tell you if the planets are in alignment for this venture of yours."

"Thanks, but I'll pass," said Donna.

"Let me know if you change your mind. I'd be happy to do it. One good turn deserves another, you know. Bye now. Thanks again!"

Donna hung up the phone and slumped heavily onto the kitchen stool. Is that how the neighbors perceive me? A Hausfrau? A church lady? A frumpy room mother? Maybe Margo's right, she thought. Maybe I do hide my light under a bushel. Maybe Sister Monson is right. Maybe I am an unwise servant. She held up Nate's dirty breakfast spoon and checked her filmy reflection. "Time to make something of yourself," she said firmly.

She got out the phone book and looked up a number. Not Betty's Curl Up and Dye where she usually went to get a trim but Fernando's Salon. She dialed. "Hi. I need an appointment. It's an emergency. Do you have any openings today? Great, I'll be there in 20 minutes."

When she emerged from Fernando's, she felt like a new woman. Now no one would mistake her for a frumpy Hausfrau. Well, if they looked from the neck up, anyway. Her scattered gray hairs were extinct—each one a sultry auburn like the rest of her newly chic mane. It was a color Fernando called vixen brown. His other suggestion had been "come hither cola," which didn't appeal. The cut involved bangs, which she hadn't had since high school, and a layered, asymmetric style that would take some getting used to.

"Look out, world, here I come!" she whispered to herself as she pushed open the door to the local Filene's. She located the Lancome counter and let the youthful clerk try out various shades of gloss and shadow, highlight and accent on her face. Holding up the mirror, she liked what she saw. She wasn't exactly sure *who* it was she saw, but she liked her.

This is someone who knows she's going somewhere, she mused. This is a confident face, a 'can do' face, and beyond that, a *stylish* face! No light under the bushel for this gal!

Driving home, she justified the weight of the make-up by

33

the lighter-weight hairdo. It all balances, she told herself. But somehow, she didn't feel balanced. She felt like she'd been tossed into the spin cycle.

When the boys returned from school, Simon slipped into his accustomed spot at the computer in the family room. Nate and Ben took one look at their mother and cried. "Mom, what did you do to your head?" shrieked seven-year-old Ben. Nate, trying to be brave, moaned, "I want my mom back."

"It's me, it's me, you know it's me," she said. She tried to muffle chuckles in sympathetic tones. "I'm not going anywhere. It's just me, your regular old mom!"

"You're scary!" Ben shouted.

Donna held him tight. Maybe she had been a little radical. Maybe the color, the cut, the cosmetics were a bit much to hit them with all at once.

Then Stephanie walked in. She'll approve, Donna thought. She's been after me to spark it up for months.

"Good Heavens, Mom," said Stephanie, her jaw sagging. She tossed her backpack onto the kitchen counter. "What were you thinking?"

Stephanie yanked a hairbrush out of her pack and started in on Donna's hair. "This color is nearly purple, Mom. Yuck, they put all this spray and mousse and junk in your hair. It'll take hours to wash this out. You should have done something that makes you look your age, not like a twenty-something wannabe. Hold still, Mom. Let me fix you. Let me try, anyway. I've got to get that gunk off your face. You're always telling me not to wear so much make-up, even though it would look okay on me; on you, Mother, it's embarrassing." The younger boys wiped their tears and dashed off to watch TV, reassured that their sister would set everything back in order.

"Making you over is not a task for amateurs!" huffed Stephanie, screwing caps on small jars of creams and emollients spilling from her satchel. "When it comes to image, Mom, you can't trust your own instincts!" She stood back and squinted at Donna from a distance. "I hope I got to you in time. It's the best I can do." She shook her head and walked upstairs to her bedroom.

Donna sat there on the stool, dizzy and bewildered. *She* thought she had looked good. *She* had felt confident and stylish for the first time in months. But here in the bosom of her family, it blew up in her face. Her visage scared her sons to tears. It sent her daughter into triage mode.

She staggered to the powder room and closed the door. In the mirror, it was her old face—emphasis on old, she thought. No more eye shadow. No more lip gloss. Her cheeks were rosy, but that was because Stephanie had scrubbed them so hard that Donna thought she must be using steel wool. Her hair was still the lush vixen brown Fernando had blessed her with. She didn't care what the kids said. She *liked* the color. She held up a mirror to check out how the back of her head looked. There were still some vestiges of Fernando's do, but Stephanie had neutralized the asymmetry with her frantic brushing.

Mostly Donna just looked disheveled like she did when she got out of bed in the morning. She looked into the mirrors and saw her timeless reflections backwards and forwards, on and on into eternity. Stephanie's words echoed on and on as well: "You can't trust your own instincts, you can't trust your own instincts, you can't trust your own instincts ..."

7

By the time Hank got home that night, Donna had showered the mousse out of her hair and tried to brush it into something acceptable. It must have worked since Hank didn't comment at all.

"So, what's your itinerary for tomorrow?" he asked, forking up some peas at dinner.

"I got a fax with the details. I'm meeting with Gloria and Lucy, then they'll show me around their office and introduce me around. It's all Greek to me," said Donna.

"You don't sound as peppy as when I left this morning. Are you sure you want to do this?" Hank asked.

"Of course she wants to do this, Dad," Simon said. "She wants to make money so we can go to Disney World."

"Disney World? Really, Mom?" said Ben.

"No, Simon's teasing," said Stephanie, shoving Simon's elbow off the table. "Mom's just going to sign a contract tomorrow. Probably nothing will come of it."

"Thank you for the confidence, Steph," Donna said. "Can't you have a little enthusiasm for me?"

"Yeah, Stephanie," said Hank. "Tomorrow is a big day. You don't have to be such a wet blanket."

"Just a realist, Dad," said Stephanie. "It's Mom, remember? I mean, I love you and everything, but a celebrity? I don't think so."

"Hey, let's remember what they're promoting. It's not me, it's the oil. Does anyone hawk Bill Gates? No, it's his product."

"And we're all grateful for that," laughed Hank. "Dessert?" The conversation drifted off into details about spelling tests and who needed new shoes and whose turn it was to mow the lawn. Donna felt her equilibrium returning.

Tuesday morning she shooed the kids out the door to school. Margo arrived at 7:45 to drive her to the airport.

"Love your hair!" Margo said when Donna climbed into the car. "And look at the earrings! They actually show up! I like your hair short!"

"Thanks," Donna said. "You seem to be the only one on the planet who does."

"What do you mean? Don't you like it?" Margo said.

"Oh, gee, Margo," Donna sighed. "What do I know about what I like?"

"Oh, cut it out. You're going to New York City to knock 'em dead and sell a million bottles of that brew, and you know you like the whole adventure of it!" Margo said.

"You sound sure enough for both of us," Donna said.

"Of course I am!" Margo chirped. "Any right thinking person would like this! It's the chance of a lifetime! You're going to shine!"

Donna remembered why she liked Margo. The pep talks, the infusion of good will, the ever-optimistic point of view. She was the medicine Donna needed this morning. A vitamin for a sagging ego.

When they pulled up at the curb at Logan Airport, Margo pulled up the brake, dashed around to the other side of the car, and gave Donna a big hug.

"You promise to tell me every detail! Every single detail! You can't leave anything out!"

"I love you, Margo," Donna said. She waved as the automatic doors opened.

"Love you, too!" Margo shouted. "As they say at Girls Camp, remember who you are!"

The plane ride was an experience. Donna had flown before but had never been ushered onto the plane first. She had never sat in a seat expansive enough to be a La-Z-Boy. She had never had flight attendants put a little napkin on her lap and serve her soda pop and pretzels before the plane even took off. Wow! It was only an hour flight, but it was as relaxing as being at a spa.

When she got off the plane at Kennedy Airport, she was surprised to see a young man in a dark suit holding up a sign with her name on it. Why does that security man have my name on a sign? she thought. Then panic set in. Something happened to one of the kids. They've been trying to reach me and I wasn't there. Now one of them's hurt, and here I am, gallivanting off to the big city when one of my kids or my husband ... Oh, no! What if it's Hank! What if something happened to him!?

"I'm Donna Brooks," she said, clutching the arm of the young man with the sign. "What's wrong? Who's hurt?"

The man looked at her oddly. "Ma'am, I'm just here to give you a ride to Big Apple's offices. Are you okay?"

Donna felt her heart rate drop back to normal. She blushed at her naiveté. Straightening herself up, she let go of the man's sleeve and cleared her throat. "Oh, I'm fine, fine. Just a little turbulence," she said. She followed the chauffeur. She tried to look like she did this sort of thing every day. There were hundreds of suited executives rushing about, many of them on cell phones. Some were waiting for outgoing planes and clicking away at laptop computers. She felt like Dorothy in the land of Oz.

It wasn't as if she was a hick off the turnip truck. She lived outside of Boston, for heaven's sake. But the only one in the family who ever wore a suit was Hank, and the only reason she ever went downtown was to chaperone a school field trip to the aquarium. Usually it was blue jeans and t-shirts, not pantyhose and pinstripes.

Who am I kidding? I should turn around right now and go home! she thought on the elevator up to the thirty-fifth floor. Then to her surprise, she felt a soothing confidence come to her. It was almost literally words in her ear: This is a chance of a lifetime! Go on, Donna! Relax! Enjoy yourself! I'll be with you! Don't worry! Have a ball! Kick butt!

It must be Margo's voice, she figured, since she doubted the Spirit would use words like kick butt. Still, she followed the instructions. When the doors opened on the thirty-fifth floor, she was indeed relaxed. Her smile was genuine. She felt comfortable in her stylish earrings and her vixen brown hair.

"Donna, you look lovely!" Gloria gushed. She was waiting at the reception desk. "Lucy will be with us in just a minute or two. She's got the contract for you. Given that we're already coming up on September, there's really not a moment to lose getting this launched. As it is, we printed up some dummies for advertising flyers. Come along with me and I'll show you what we have in mind. There are a couple styles to choose from. We want you to take a look."

Donna wanted to say something, even hello, but there didn't seem to be an appropriate time. Already Gloria had her by the elbow and was walking her briskly down a hallway. The walls were lined with huge photos of products Donna recognized. There was quite a range from tires to toilet paper.

"Okay, here we go. Right this way!" Gloria said. They peeled off into a room on the left. There before her were two tilt-top design desks with tall stools and a light oak conference table and modern chairs in brilliant hues all around it. Easels with covered panels stood by the dry erase board. The far wall was a floor-to-ceiling window looking over Manhattan.

"This is so gorgeous!" gasped Donna. She looked out over the city. When she saw just how high up they were, she had to steady herself.

"It really is majestic, isn't it?" Gloria agreed. "Yep, the Big Apple in all its glory. And you're going to take a bite!"

"Hi, Donna!" said Lucy Hobbes, walking in.

Gloria gushed: "Lucy, Lucy, Lucy! Glad you're here. I can't wait to unveil the dummies!"

Donna wasn't sure what "unveil the dummies" referred to. An exotic dance?

"First things first," said Lucy. "Let's get these contracts signed. Our legal department assures me they're just the standard contract. Here you go!" She handed Donna a pen.

"This is so exciting!" said Donna, scrawling her signature at the bottom of the last page where the little sticky tab indicated.

"Now that that's behind us, let's get started," said Gloria, launching into another nonstop stream of words. "Like I said, Donna, this is the Big Apple where everything's due yesterday. Have we got plans for you! First, we're tossing around some ideas for the product. Lucy's good with facts and figures, but the ideas!

39

Well, the ideas are my *pied de terre*. So, we've come up with a good name for the product."

"My husband and I had some thoughts," began Donna.

"Well, just leave that to us, dear," Gloria broke in. "You're the genius who made the stuff. We're the ones who are going to market it. You brought the recipe, right?"

"Yes," said Donna. She pulled a piece of paper out of her handbag.

"Wonderful," said Gloria, snatching it out of her hands. "We'll get our chemists working on this right away." She pressed a button on the desk phone and asked for a page to come to pick up the recipe.

"Now take a look at these goodies. You'll want to see this, too, Lucy. Let me know which one you think will attract the most attention." With that she yanked the covers off the panels on two easels.

Donna gasped. One was of a woman dressed in a long leather blacksmith's bibbed apron—*only* an apron. Behind her, a huge foundry oven glowed like the fires of hell. The caption read, "Spark up your life with Sinnamon!"

The other panel showed a curvy peaches-and-cream-complexioned homemaker in the kitchen holding a pan of cinnamon rolls. She too was wearing an apron—over a skimpy mini-skirt and tube-top. The caption read, "You'll never forget those buns ... with Sinnamon!"

Donna stared at the panels in stunned silence for several long seconds. Then she exploded. "NO WAY!" she shouted. "I'm sorry, but these are not acceptable! There is simply no way! You can *not* use my product and turn it into some ... come-on juice!"

Gloria was unruffled. "Donna, we all know your oil leaves rhino's horns in the dust. You think we're not going to play that up for all it's worth? Get real. You're in the big leagues now." She seemed amused at Donna's reaction.

Donna looked to Lucy for support, but Lucy was still studying the panels. "Gloria, I, uh, understand you're trying to tap the market, but I think you've overlooked some of the other attributes Donna's product has," she stammered.

"Yeah, yeah—hearth, home and all that. I know, I know. That's the thing that grabs you first. But does *that* sell? Not like you-know-what. Anyway, that's what we were after in the Susie Homemaker shot anyway."

"Haven't you ever heard of subtlety?" Donna screeched. "This is ridiculous. I'm sorry, but if this is the only thing you can come up with to sell this, I'm out of here."

"Hey there, girl," Gloria said cooly, examining her fingernails. "We've got a signed contract, remember?"

"The ink's not even dry!" Donna shouted.

"We could still sue you," Gloria chortled.

"Sure, go ahead! But there is no way I will let you pair my oil with smut!" Suddenly Donna remembered the phone number Sister Monson had given her. "I'm getting a lawyer!" she stated. She ruffled through her handbag and found Sister Monson's number, grabbed the phone, and started dialing.

"I'm sure we can work out some kind of compromise here," said Lucy. "Gloria, frankly I'm embarrassed by these, too. Maybe Donna's right. Maybe we should go back to the drawing board."

"You're not getting soft on me now, are you, Lucy?" Gloria laughed. Then she saw that Donna was speaking to someone on the phone.

"A friend of mine has arranged to send a lawyer. He's on his way," Donna said, hanging up the phone. "We'll get this straightened out. And for pity's sake, cover up those obscene pictures."

Gloria took a step back, put her hands on her hips, and just eyed Donna for a long awkward minute. "I've got it! A whole new approach!" Gloria finally trumpeted. She came up to Donna, put her arm around her and looked her directly in the eye. "Lady," she said. "You are it! *You* will sell this stuff!

41

"What are you talking about" asked Donna warily, slipping herself out of the chummy contact.

"You are really something else. You come in here looking all warm-hearted and then, WHAM! Look at you! As good old Helen Reddy used to say, 'Hear me roar!' You are a lioness! Sort of like Joan of Arc in a car pool. Once you hook them into the power of that smell, it's Joan of Arc, car pool, and Mae West."

"What do you mean 'I will sell this stuff'? I've never done any retail in my life unless you call selling hot dogs at a Little League game retail," Donna said nervously. "And Mae West? Take another look, honey."

Gloria burst out laughing. "I love it! You are the real thing, aren't you! You know, Lucy, we could have had casting work on this for months and they'd never have found anyone quite so perfect for this product!"

Gloria circled around Donna, looking her up and down. She kept talking to Lucy. "She's really not someone to mess with but approachable at the same time, don't you think? I think that's terrific! I think, in fact, that *that's* what this scent is all about, don't you? Power *and* comfort. Tenderness *and* va-va-voom vitality!"

"I see what you mean, Gloria," Lucy said. "What do you think, Donna?"

"I'm a little lost here," Donna admitted.

"We'd have to do something—an apron, maybe? Foxier hair? More make-up?"

Gloria lifted a lock of Donna's hair. "Gotta get that combo balanced just right."

"You mean you want me to be in ads for the oil?" Donna asked. "Me?"

"That's right! We'll capture your essence just like you've captured the essence of that cinnamony stuff. Mix those up together and I think we've got a recipe for success," Gloria chuckled.

"Will I have to talk? Or will this just be photos, or what?

I'm not that big on public speaking and I'm not very photogenic. My kids could tell you that," Donna began. She felt shy at the prospect but exhilarated at the same time. She had known a few people who did commercials and they made terrific money. Maybe that trip to Disney World would be possible after all! This was turning out to be better than she had imagined! And to think she had just about ripped up the papers and walked out. Everything was happening so fast!

At that moment, the attorney Roger Frost appeared. "Which one of you is Donna Brooks?"

Donna raised her hand.

Mr. Frost turned to the other women. "Will you excuse us? I need to discuss some legal matters with Ms. Brooks."

"Yeah, yeah, fine," muttered Gloria. "But don't take too long. We've got a deadline."

When they were alone, Mr. Frost explained that Sister Monson told him all about the situation, that he understood how to help her. Did she want him to represent her? Yes. Did she want clauses promising, oh say, artistic veto power on advertising? Absolutely! How about a consultant provided by the church's Public Affairs Department? Sounds great. With some scratching here and initials there, Mr. Frost transformed the original contract.

Donna still wasn't sure what all the clauses meant, but she knew that she could now personally veto any lurid advertising. Mr. Frost explained some of the more foreign terms, but his explanations sounded like gobbledy-gook. She knew he was a friend of Sister Monson, and that took away all her worries. Ah, the comfort of the fellowship of the Saints!

There were some confusing new lines about promotional tours and appearances which Mr. Frost assured her was *pro forma* for such arrangements.

"I appreciate your help with this," said Donna as the attorney collected his paperwork.

"These legal issues always involve compromise of some kind

43

or another," Mr. Frost said. "I think, all things considered, they didn't get away with too much. Congratulations. That's quite a coup."

"Thanks, I guess," said Donna. "But what do you mean exactly. What *did* they get away with?"

Mr. Frost exhaled deeply. Donna read that as Lady, are you dense? What you really need is someone to hold your hand. He turned the corners of his mouth up into something approximating a smile. "I just mean, I think it was gracious of you to concede on the name. It seems a small sacrifice, given how much involvement you're going to have."

"What do you mean, concede on the name?" Donna's pulse quickened.

"Sinnamon—with an S," Mr. Frost said. "That's the name they're insisting on."

"You're kidding," Donna sighed.

"Mrs. Brooks, it's right there in the first paragraph." He pointed to some convoluted clauses and tapped his finger impatiently on the paper. "I explained this to you earlier." Donna sensed a snarl coming.

"Fine, fine. As you say, compromises have to be made sometimes," she said wanly. "Thanks again for your help."

8

Hank picked up Donna at the airport at 9:00 p.m., and she fell asleep on the ride home. Somehow she staggered into the house and into pajamas and into bed, but retained no memory of it. When she woke up Wednesday morning, Hank had already gone to work. This was the normal order of things, and Donna was usually glad not to have one more person to deal with on a school morning, as much as she loved the man. But today, after the kids were off, she gave him a call at the office.

"Hi there, handsome," she sighed deeply into the phone when he answered.

"Who's calling, please?" he teased. "You were out like a light! I hardly got a word out of you about your day in the big city! You mumbled something in your sleep, though."

"Really?" asked Donna. "What did I say?"

"It didn't make any sense. Something about leather aprons."

Donna laughed. She gave Hank a brief recap.

"Sinnamon, huh?" Hank said. "If you just say it and don't do it, it's fine with me. Let me get this straight. They're using *you* in their ads?"

"Yeah, that's what they said."

"And when does all this start?"

"Just a second, Hank," Donna said. "There's another call coming in." She put him on hold. "Hello?"

"Hi—just waiting for my lunch. We've got you set up for a couple of photo shoots. One here on Friday in New York and then we thought we'd take some at your home on Sunday. Got the first batch of Sinnamon from the chemists. Wonderful stuff! I'll fax you the facts and figures. Oh, goody—here's the waiter ... "

Donna recognized Gloria's voice. Good thing, since she hung up without identifying herself. Donna picked up Hank again.

"That was fast," he said.

"I can't believe it," Donna said. "That was Gloria. I've got to be back in New York on Friday for some kind of photo shoot, and they're coming here on Sunday to take more pictures."

"They don't waste any time, do they?" Hank said.

"I'm still worn out from yesterday. Will I be revived by Friday?"

"Oh, just go do something relaxing. Wax the floors or something," he teased.

"Very funny! Seriously, start thinking about what kind of holiday you'd like when this is all over. They sound pretty encouraging about how well this is going to sell. Oops, sorry honey, there's another call on the line."

"You really are in demand, aren't you?" said Hank. "I'll just sign off. See you tonight. Love you."

"Love you, too." She clicked for the other call.

"Hello, Donna. This is Juliet Benton, your new visiting teaching companion," said Juliet.

"Juliet, of course!" said Donna. "Glad you called. Visiting teaching? Yes. I've got some obligations Friday, but any time tomorrow morning looks okay. Do you want me to call our ladies or do you want to set it up?"

Juliet volunteered to do the arranging. A half hour later she called back with three out of four appointments scheduled for the next morning.

It will be such a relief to spend time on the Lord's work, Donna thought. She started humming "As Sisters in Zion" and felt the weight of Big Apple slip off her shoulders.

Thursday morning Juliet came by and they drove to Cindy Borden's house. Cindy was a young housewife who had been in the Boston area for three years now. Donna was assigned to her when she and her husband first arrived from Pocatello with a tiny baby. "We're just here for business school," she said in her lilting girlish voice. Donna had noticed the calendar in the kitchen with big red Xs on it. Thinking it might have something to do with fertility, she didn't ask about it. But Cindy volunteered right up front that this was her "countdown to happiness" calendar. She could endure her time here by checking off each day. Each red X brought her one day closer to Zion, to life as she knew it, and as she intended to have again. "Endure to the end" was cross stitched on a couch pillow.

Just when Cindy's twins were born, her husband announced that he was taking a job in the Boston area, not back in Idaho.

This called for some serious hand-holding. Poor Cindy came close to losing it. Now the twins were a year and a half old, and Cindy still tried to sound perky, but there was an edginess that hadn't been there in the early years.

"Hi, Cindy," Donna said when Cindy opened the door. "Do you know my new companion, Juliet Benton?"

"Hi, sisters!" said Cindy, opening the door and welcoming them in. "I just got the twins down for a nap and Brittany is at preschool. I'm taking her in two mornings a week this year, so I have about an hour of peace and quiet. Back in Pocatello, I could have called my mom, and she'd have been here in ten seconds. But that's just not how it works here. I suppose preschool is the best I can do. Out in Pocatello, no one would do that, you know. My mother-in-law still doesn't know. I hope in the long run, the Lord will forgive us because of the sacrifices we've had to make. You don't think I've sold my soul, do you?"

Juliet sat down on the couch where Cindy had collapsed and took Cindy's hand. "The Lord knows how much you love your children, Cindy," Juliet said. "I'm sure He understands how eager you are to do the right thing."

"You think?" Cindy said, her eyes starting to brim with tears.

"I'm sure of it, Cindy," Juliet said.

They had planned to give a lesson and chit chat a bit, but Donna was hit with a powerful impulse that she couldn't resist. "I'm sure of it, too, Cindy," she said. "And I have the strongest sense that the best thing we can do for you is to let you get some sleep for the next hour while the twins are napping."

"You think?" Cindy said again. "I mean, is that okay? I actually didn't get any sleep last night. Brigham has a cold. A nap would be great, but are you sure that's okay? Shouldn't I be getting a message from the *Ensign* or something?"

"Cindy, I'm afraid you'll have to settle for a message from the Spirit. The Spirit is saying you need to nap and we need to go.

It's so strong that I could almost write a hymn about it. So we'll be going now." Donna got up and moved toward the door.

"Goodbye, Cindy," Juliet said. "I'll look forward to meeting the kids soon. I'll give you a call."

"That was unusual," Donna said when they were back in the car. "I think we set some kind of record for the shortest visiting teaching." Their next appointment wasn't for another forty-five minutes, so they pulled into McDonald's and got some drinks.

"How old is Cindy? She looks young," asked Juliet. "So young, and so tired."

"I think she's about twenty-three," Donna said.

"Why did she keep asking if it would be okay? Who decides these kinds of things if not her?"

"She's pretty young. And she's had a sheltered life," Donna mused. "We see a lot of newcomers like that. It's kind of a strange phenomenon, like one of those Oprah show topics. Women Who Need Permission."

Juliet chuckled softly. "That's never been one of *my* problems."

This caught Donna by surprise. Juliet was not shy like some of the younger women in the ward, but she didn't strike Donna as an Outta My Way, Here I Come type either.

"Tell me about that," said Donna.

"It's just not how I was raised. My mother was a dynamic woman. Lots of traveling. Lots of public speaking engagements for the Women's League. There was nothing she couldn't accomplish once she set her mind to it. She expected the same from her children. My sister and brother and I were always taught that life gives us challenges and our task is to do the most with what we've got—with what happens to us. She really put that into practice when she was diagnosed with breast cancer. She lived four months after the diagnosis."

"How awful," Donna said sympathetically. "I'm sorry. What about your dad? Where was he during all of this?"

"My dad was my mother's biggest booster. He had a lot of his own business obligations, but he went into semi-retirement when Mom got ill and he did most of his work from home. This, of course, was in the days before computers, so it was trickier then. But we're a determined lot, the Bentons."

"Sounds like it. How did your family feel about you joining the church?"

Juliet was silent for a while, sipping her soda. "My dad and sister thought I'd lost my mind. My brother was more understanding, but even he was puzzled. Frankly, I was puzzled, too, at first."

"What do you mean?"

"The church has an image, you know. Very conservative. None of us fits that description. For example, I don't think there's ever been a Republican in our family, even though we're technically descendants of the *Mayflower*. But our forefather, Eli Fogg, wasn't the reverent type. He was one of the deck hands. Seems he ran off with one of the natives. When she died in childbirth, he brought the baby back to Plimoth Plantation. But then he died—probably of a venereal disease he brought from England. The boy was raised by one of the other families."

"That's an interesting genealogy! You should be the spotlight sister so you can share that gem!" Donna laughed. "But you were saying you were puzzled about joining the church."

"Yes," Juliet continued. "You know how you felt compelled to leave Cindy so she could take a nap?"

"Sure."

"Something like that, but with higher voltage. Remember that boy I told you about who had CTR carved into his haircut? I contacted LDS Social Services to help him out, and I ended up meeting a stake missionary. Out of courtesy, I agreed to listen to the missionary lessons. One night when I was praying for the welfare of that young boy, something grabbed me. It's hard to describe. It wasn't a voice. It wasn't my first experience with any-

49

thing spiritual. I was raised Unitarian, you know, and despite what some might think, they can be very spiritual." Juliet laughed a little.

"Go on," Donna urged.

"But something more powerful and emphatic told me to join the Mormon church. Nobody, not even my dad, was more surprised than I was. In a quiet little service, my friend, the stake missionary, baptized me in a lake in Ithaca early one Sunday morning. Since that time, a year and a half ago, I've learned that some experiences are too large for words."

She continued: "This is hard to communicate to my dad who loves words. He's a killer Scrabble player. He does the *New York Times* crossword puzzle every Sunday without fail. He keeps pressing me to explain this to him. It's frustrating since I pride myself on vocabulary. It's tricky to see aspects of church culture that I did *not* seek out that I can't defend."

"Like what?" Donna asked.

"Well, like I said, the squeaky clean, straight-laced image, for one thing. It drives my dad crazy!" Juliet glanced at her watch. "Goodness, Donna! I've talked on so long! We've got five minutes to get to our next appointment!"

"We'd better get a move on," Donna said. Squeaky clean image. Wasn't that exactly what Sister Monson wanted to be sure she would peddle? How could it be that the very image that attracted some people repelled others? Maybe Juliet's father didn't have his heart in the right place.

They arrived at Patty Dominico's house a couple minutes late. Patty was a long-time convert born and raised in the Boston area. She greeted them with hugs. "Come on in, ladies!" she said cheerfully. "I've got some cannolis for you at the table. Come, eat! Eat!"

The half hour passed quickly with stories about Patty's grandchildren and a little complaining about her newly retired husband who hung around the house too much. Periodically,

Patty said, "Eat! Eat! You there, Juliet, you're too skinny! Gotta get some meat on your bones!" Donna and Juliet headed off to their third appointment well fed.

The next visit was to Ellen Young, a matronly great-something-granddaughter of Brigham Young. She was disaffected from the church and only begrudgingly allowed visiting teachers to come. "I've got to be out of here in twenty minutes," she announced coolly as she held open the door for Juliet and Donna.

"Hi, Ellen," Donna began. "This is my new companion, Juliet Benton. She teaches art history at Brandeis."

"Where'd you get your degree?" Ellen asked, getting right to the point. For a daughter of the Utah Pioneers, Ellen had the abrasive edge of a native Yankee. Juliet didn't seem put off.

"My Ph.D. is from Cornell," she said. "My B.A. is from Bates."

"Bates?" said Ellen, brightening. "I went to Bates, class of '51."

"Great abolitionist tradition there," Juliet said proudly. "A wonderful place for free thinkers."

"Yes," said Ellen cautiously. The limited conversation veered to Ellen's hot-house orchids and her volunteer time with the Audubon Society. "Time for you to leave," she said when twenty minutes had past. But as Donna and Juliet were getting into the car, Ellen called out, "I'll see you next month."

It wasn't even halfway through the month and three out of four visiting teaching assignments were already done! Only one more sister to visit—Margo.

As Donna walked into the house, she heard the phone ringing. She ran to get it before the answering machine picked it up. "So, spill, woman!" said Margo. "Tell me every detail! I'm on my lunch hour. You can tell me all about it!"

9

"You're on your lunch hour? If I'd known, we would have come over and visited you, too," said Donna. "Well, let's see. Ellen Young was more hospitable than she's ever been. Seemed to take a shine to Juliet. And Juliet is fascinating! I got the oddest urge at Cindy Borden's to let Cindy ... "

"No, not that, you ninny!" interrupted Margo. "I want the lowdown on your New York trip!"

"Oh, that!" said Donna. She gave Margo the highlights.

"And they're coming out this weekend to interview you?" Margo gushed. "And you're going back on Friday? Are you sure I can't come with you?"

"Sorry, Margo. I wish you could. I could use your enthusiasm. Some of these people are so worldly, it makes me uncomfortable. I'm not wild about them coming on Sunday, either. I like our quiet little regimen on Sundays—well, as quiet as four kids will let you be."

Margo laughed. "Hey, I think you should have gone with the black leather apron thing. If I were twenty years younger and twenty pounds lighter, I'd volunteer to be their model. What's the gripe about worldly anyway? Aren't we told to be 'in the world'? Isn't that what the scriptures say?"

"Gee, Margo," said Donna. "Don't tell me you've forgotten the last part of that quote."

"What last part?" Margo asked.

"The 'but not of it' part!"

"Oh, details!" Margo laughed. "Of course. I know, I know, but don't be so uptight that you let this opportunity slip you by."

"I just told you I'm having a photo shoot on Friday and a camera crew is coming on Sunday."

"You need to loosen up and relax," Margo said. "Oops, Dr. Costelli's wandering down the hall with a stack of insurance forms. I better get out of here. If he sees me, there goes my lunch hour! Love ya! CALL ME!"

Donna took Margo's advice on Friday and relaxed on the plane. She relaxed when the limo guy picked her up and relaxed in the elevator. She was so relaxed that she nearly fell asleep when the make-over crew washed her hair in the sink. After the hair coloring and styling, she was whisked off for a make-up session.

"What do you think?" asked Maddy, the make-up stylist. Maddy stepped to the side so Donna could see herself full-face in the mirror. "I think it captures the look Gloria had in mind."

Donna loved her new look. She looked younger and more chic but not like the Generation-X wannabe that Stephanie would laugh at. Her hair color was worlds better than the vixen brown she'd loved just a week ago. The little adjustments to the home-town haircut made a surprising difference. And the make-up! Color in all the right places, cover-up on all the others. A little gloss here, a little powder there.

"I feel like one of Oprah's make-over show success stories!" gushed Donna. "I'll never be able to reproduce this."

"Oh, but you won't need to. We'll be there whenever you're having a TV interview and when you're on tour. That's the way Gloria wants it. We'll be spending a lot of time together over the next month or two. Just leave your looks to us. Your head is in our hands!" Maddy laughed.

"Yes, yes, of course ... " Donna said absently. She was so distracted by the new and improved version of herself in the mirror that she wasn't paying close attention to Maddy.

"Time's flying," bellowed a thin, middle-aged man, clapping his hands as he entered. He was followed by a short Asian woman in her early twenties. "Wardrobe time! I'm Rico and I'll be coordinating your clothing. Let's see, what shall we go with? ..."

Donna began to answer, about to tell him she had brought some things from home.

"Shush, dear. You've got to let me concentrate," he said

53

brusquely. He circled around her, staring at her from crown to toe. He moved the chair around from left to right, right to left, observing her in all her angles.

"Okay, we'll go with turquoise linen—a tailored jacket and a simple tank top underneath. Peach or salmon tone, a good complimentary color. Nothing funereal. Tidy but stylish, then jazz it up with some simple accessory. A scarf for flair. Don't want to look stuffy. Okay, Lisa? Fetch." He snapped his fingers and the young woman left. She returned momentarily with arm loads of clothing matching Rico's requests.

"Okay, dear," said Rico. "Careful of the face now. The make-up's just right. Time to try these on." Donna waited for him to leave.

"Come on, honey. Get a move on. You need a hand with that thing you're wearing?" Rico snapped. "Off with it!"

Donna had only heard this kind of attitude from sassy children. She was not about to put up with it here. "Look—Rico, is it?" Donna said in a steely, no-nonsense tone. "You're going to have to leave now if you want me to try these on."

Rico looked dumbfounded. "Get over it, honey," he said. "I'm not here for my jollies. There's no time to tiptoe around."

"You listen to me, honey," Donna barked back. "No way am I going to drop my trousers in front of you." She could feel her lioness surging. "There is some stuff about my clothing that you wouldn't get, and I'm not in a mood to go into with you. You can forget the tank top, too. Get me something with sleeves."

"Unacceptable" said Rico fiercely.

"Unacceptable or not, I *do not* wear tank tops and I am not going to discuss it with *you*. I don't like your attitude, mister." Her tone was icy. By the time she got to the "mister" part, she was out of the make-up chair, standing and staring him directly in the eye, inches from his face.

Rico huffed and let the door slam behind him, muttering

something about "the bossy diva." Lisa opened the door and crept out timidly behind him.

Donna felt tickles of guilt nibbling at her. Did she have to speak to him so snippily? Couldn't she have handled him with more Christian charity? No, she decided. You can't let snotty know-it-alls run right over you. When it comes to privacy and clothing—and garments—she was not going to be bullied by some little tyrant. Hey, maybe it was one of those "reproving be-times with sharpness" experiences.

The door opened just then. Gloria came in laughing and clapping. "Bravo, Donna! You've done what no one has dared do before—talk back to royal Rico. He's not used to being told off. Frankly, Donna, this is so exciting! You show me the kind of stuff you're made of once again and I love it! What did I tell you? You're homespun—although that hairdo and make-up are looking stylish—homespun and smart, but then—KaPow! Just like Sinna-mon, you knock their socks off!"

Gloria was into her non-stop jabber mode and kept going. "I *knew* it was right to go with you! It's time we start planning TV interviews. We want to get the product into a few stores in a cou-ple of weeks, and I think we ought to get you onto *Good Morning America* right after that."

"*Good Morning America?*" stammered Donna.

"You're a natural. Anyway, I'm tight with Michael Eisner. I'll drop a vial of Sinnamon over at his house tomorrow, and I'm sure it will happen. *Good Morning America* for sure. Don't know if we can get Oprah. She does a lot of taping in Chicago, of all places. L. A. I could understand, but Chicago? What is the woman think-ing? Well, if it works, it works, and clearly the girl's workin' it. Now, about the clothes. We'll make adjustments within reason and let you have privacy as long as it's speedy. I haven't got a clue why you turned down a tank top. Do you know how hot it gets under those lights?"

Donna found out soon enough. During the afternoon photo

shoot, she got talced down by the make-up staff every fifteen minutes. She started to cast a few damp shadows on the linen jacket, too, and Rico sullenly produced a lavender, short-sleeved sheath as an alternative. Her favorite of all the ensembles was an emerald green number they put her in. She asked if she could keep the outfits. No, they said.

She found herself comfortable in front of the camera, except for the heat. The photographer was a spunky woman about Donna's mother's age. Lois Wheaton set her right at ease. Taking shot after shot, she chattered away about her days as a camp counselor, her love for the *Antiques Roadshow* on TV, her start in photography at age fifty when a shot she took of Whoopi Goldberg on Martha's Vineyard caught Big Apple's eye.

"You've been to Martha's Vineyard?" Donna asked, the camera click-click-clicking away. "I've always wanted to go. We're so close, but I've never been."

"That, my dear, is something we will have to remedy!" Lois said. "I think we've got enough! Thanks, Donna. It was great working with you. I'll see you on Sunday at the site shot. That's mostly for video footage, but they want a few stills, too. Candids, you know. Maybe with some with your kids. Heck, you could use some of them for your Christmas cards."

"Wow! Thanks, Lois!" said Donna enthusiastically. "I'll look forward to seeing you Sunday!"

By the time Donna got onto the plane back to Boston, she felt like a new woman. She didn't feel like the bedraggled mother of four. She didn't feel like a PTA minion or a lowly chauffeur. She felt accomplished and capable and so pleased that something genuinely hers—her combo of "down-home" simplicity and lioness defensiveness—was appreciated by these folks. She didn't have to pretend such things. They really were her. And apparently they were marketable.

10

"Welcome, welcome, Sabbath morning!" crooned Donna as she went room to room. She dropped sections of the Sunday paper on the threshold of each bedroom. It was their Sunday ritual. Ben and Nate got the comics to fight over. Simon got the sports section. Stephanie got the magazine. Donna and Hank shared what was left, hoping that by the end of the day they could rescue at least some of the other sections.

One by one they showed up in the kitchen, grabbed the cereal of their choice or tossed a Pop-tart in the toaster if there was time before they had to leave for church. Then it was the scramble for the car.

"Get the crumbs off your face, Nate," said Donna as she buckled her seat belt. "We've got to hurry. Simon's giving the youth talk today."

"I am?" shrieked Simon. "That's the first I heard of it! Since when?"

"I told you on Tuesday, Simon," said Donna.

"You did not," insisted Simon. "You were in New York, remember? You couldn't have told me."

"Oh, my goodness," said Donna, remembering the sequence now. "When I came back from New York I checked the messages and there was a message from Brother Evans about it. I was going to write it down for you, but I was so tired I must have forgotten! I'm so sorry, Simon!"

"Well, good then. *You* can give the talk!" Simon said.

"But *I'm* not a youth speaker," Donna said. "I can't do this for you. Come on, Simon. You can come up with something. Don't tell me you would have put much more preparation into it if I had told you on time."

"That's not the point, Mom," argued Simon. "Besides, you're

the one who's going to be going public next week. You need the practice. Not me."

"That's entirely different," said Donna.

"Actually, Mom, he's got a point," Stephanie piped in. "Aren't you the one who's always talking about the consequences of our behavior?"

"Yeah, Mom, they're right," said Nate.

Ben, who hadn't been paying any attention, perked up and joined the "yeah, they're right" chorus.

"Hank, what do you think?" Donna asked, hoping for a solid line of parental defense.

"I'm not touching this one, Donna," he laughed. "When I have to fill in with a high council talk at the last minute, I can't say I'm ever happy about it."

Twenty minutes later, Donna was up behind the podium giving the youth talk. Scrambling to put thoughts together, she came up with a short message about the wise men giving their gifts to the Christ child. It wasn't Christmas, but she liked the story. Besides, it was a nice message to think of giving to Jesus all through the year. As it turned out, she talked longer than she needed to.

When she sat back down behind the bishop and his counselors, she perused the congregation while the next speaker spoke about selfless service. There was Claudia Christiansen wrestling with her toddlers as usual. There was Jane Schmidt in riveted attention. Elizabeth Potter, looking a little frail today, rested her white-haired head on the back of the bench and slept, mouth open. In the back row Donna spotted Margo, who seemed to be looking directly at her.

When she made eye contact, Margo suddenly looked like she had developed some kind of twitch. Then Margo added a pointed finger to her head twitch and Donna realized she was trying to get her to look at something. Make that some*one*. Right next to Margo sat a short, casually dressed older woman, and Donna was sure she had seen her somewhere before. But where?

It was Lois Wheaton, the photographer from New York! Donna's jaw dropped and she gasped loudly enough that the bishop turned around to look at her. She looked back at Margo, who sat there grinning broadly, very satisfied with herself.

As soon as sacrament meeting was over, Donna made her way to the back of the chapel to greet Lois. Margo was at her elbow. "Lois, what a wonderful surprise!" said Donna, hugging Lois gently.

"I hope you don't mind. I beat the rest of the team here and found your address. No one was home, of course, but then ... "

"But then I drove by on a dash to church," Margo added, leaping into the conversation. "You know me. Always last minute. And since your house is right on my route, I stopped when I saw Ms. Wheaton in your driveway."

"Margo's been quite a help," added Lois. "She told me you were here and I followed her right on in. Looks like I'm dressed down for this event. Hope that's okay."

"Of course, of course! It's just fine!" said Margo. "We're headed off to Sunday school now. Care to join us?"

"Sunday school! Sure! That sounds like fun. Haven't been to Sunday school since I was a kid," Lois said. "I surely enjoyed your meeting, Donna. Very low church. Communal. That baby in front of us kept me quite amused."

"I'm glad you're so charitable!" laughed Margo before Donna could say anything. "My impulse was to strangle that little kid," she said, looping her arm through Donna's. "Lois tells me the photo shoot is scheduled for 1:00. Of course you can count on me to be there! Well, here we are, Sunday school class."

When the teacher, Floyd Manwaring, surged into an apocalyptic view of the current troubles in the Middle East, Donna wondered if it wouldn't have been wiser to go to the Gospel Essentials class with Lois. She looked over and noticed that Lois had a little sketch book in her lap and was drawing quick sketches of people in the room. After class, a couple of people came up to introduce themselves.

"I'm Lois Wheaton, a friend of Donna's," she said simply.

Donna appreciated her sense of discretion. She could have said: "I'm Lois Wheaton, photographer of celebrities, schmoozer with the high and mighty. I shot wedding photos for Prince Edward and Sophie Rhys-Jones. I've been honored at the White House. My photos hang in the Museum of Contemporary Art." After Sunday school, Lois asked Donna if they could sit out in the foyer and get better acquainted.

"Fine with me!" said Donna.

They sat down on the orange couch beneath the picture of Christ ordaining the apostles. Lois asked her where she grew up. Born in Utah, Donna said; moved to Madison, Wisconsin, when she was five; BYU for college, where she met and married Hank; then to the Boston area where they've been living for the past seventeen years.

Donna asked Lois where she grew up. Born in Nairobi, she said. Lived there 'til she was ten, then moved to Tunis for five years. Then boarding school in Switzerland just after World War II. Fell in love with a French soldier she met on a school holiday. Married the French soldier. Divorced the French soldier a year later and vowed never to marry again. Worked at an orangutan preserve, Camp Leaky in Africa. That's where she had her camp counseling experience. Moved to Malaysia to work for the peace corps. Picked up some interesting artifacts—some of them hundreds of years old. Sold them to museums in England and the U.S., thereby her interest in the *Antiques Roadshow*. She endured a few bandit attacks in various underdeveloped countries and a few lawsuits in civilized countries and had a few romances here and there around the globe throughout her years.

"No kids," Lois added. "I think I'm simply too selfish and too much a vagabond to make a good mother. Frankly, I think be-

60

ing a mother must be the hardest job in the world. I admire you for it. I admit there have been days when I wished I had children. Right now I would love to have some grandkids I could pamper."

"You know, Lois," said Donna. "I'm surprised. When we were in New York, I thought you were so laid back, so normal."

"Does that mean you've changed your mind on that count?" laughed Lois.

"No, not at all. It's just that we were talking about TV flea markets and slopping out goulash to kids at camp and being on latrine patrol; that's my life. That's my real life. But you've got this exotic past and all these fabulous experiences. You know all these interesting people. It's going to take me a little time to get the two impressions to blend together."

"I don't think our worlds are so far apart, really," Lois said. "I like finding common ground. It doesn't matter much if we have Nairobi or Nebraska in common, does it? The fact is, we're connected on some points, and we're connected to other people on other points. We just have to find out what those are. It's like a treasure hunt. I love that!"

"Lois? Lois Wheaton? Is that you?" It was Juliet. She was coming out of the ladies' room. "I can't believe it! What are you doing here?"

"Juliet! For goodness sake!" said Lois as she stood up and embraced Juliet.

"You two know each other?" Donna asked, confused.

"Back when my mother was ill—through her Women's League," began Juliet.

"Yes, Juliet's mom and I were thick as thieves for a while. How's your dad doing?" Lois asked.

"He's great, fine," said Juliet. "I can't believe it's you! What are you doing here?"

"I've come to help Donna with some publicity for the product she invented," Lois said.

"At church?" Juliet continued.

"Just whiling away some time before a photo shoot. How about you? What's a good Unitarian girl doing in a place like this?" Lois laughed.

"I'm one of them now," Juliet said.

"You're a Mormon?"

"It's a long story. Are you going to be around for a while?" Juliet asked.

"Not much longer. We're doing the shoot this afternoon. I've got an idea," Lois said. Why don't the two of you come to my place on the Vineyard? We'll work it around your travel schedule, Donna. What do you say, you two?"

"Sounds great!" said Juliet. "Let me know when." She scribbled her number on the back side of a ward bulletin and handed it to Lois. "Just give me a call."

"And Donna can bring her husband and kids. There's plenty of room. You can stay overnight and take the ferry back the next afternoon. It'll be fun!" Lois said.

"I didn't know you had a place on Martha's Vineyard," Donna said.

"If the weather's nice, we can get out the bikes," Lois said. "What do you say, Donna?"

"It sounds wonderful. I'll have to check with Hank and the kids."

"Of course. We'll talk about it later."

"I've got to get back to Relief Society," Juliet said. "They asked me to say the closing prayer. Great to see you, Lois!"

"Relief Society? What's that?" asked Lois. "Is it a service group? That would fit Juliet, all right. She's quite a girl. A lot like her mother."

"It's our women's group," Donna said. "There are just a few minutes left."

Lois looked at her watch. "Tell you what. I'd love to, but right now I think I'll go into town and grab a bite to eat before the camera crew arrives."

"Oh, please, Lois," said Donna. "Why don't you just come home and have lunch with us? If you want to take some candids, you won't get more candid than that!"

"You're sure?" Lois asked.

"Absolutely!" Donna said. "Besides, you're the first living proof my kids will have that I'm doing something in New York and not just off shopping with Gloria."

"Gloria—she's something, isn't she?" Lois laughed. "Okay, count me in. But let me do something in the kitchen. It'll make me feel useful."

"Watch what you say. I may take you up on it," Donna said. Just then, Donna heard a voice behind her, the soothing voice of Sister Monson.

"Sister Brooks," she began. "I'm so pleased to meet you face to face. I'm Meredith Monson, stake Public Affairs director." Sister Monson looked to be in her mid-fifties. She had perfectly coiffed hair and her make-up was exquisite. (Donna was paying increasing attention to such things.) She wore a red suit that said Salt Lake City high society. She must have been striking in her younger days, Donna thought. She noticed a sparkling rock and band on Sister Monson's wedding finger that probably required daily calisthenics just to hold up. The manicure was perfect, the teeth flawless, and the voice—that milk and honey voice!

"Oh yes, oh yes! Sister Monson!" said Donna. "This is Lois Wheaton. She's a photographer from Big Apple, here to help with a photo shoot this afternoon."

Sister Monson extended her hand. "So pleased to meet you! A photo shoot this afternoon? Here at the church building? How wonderful!"

"Well, no," said Donna. "It's going to be at our house. A Happy Homemaker at home theme," she added lamely.

"On a Sabbath afternoon? What a wonderful choice," said Sister Monson. "Mr. Frost, the lawyer, told me how things went. Sounds like a great situation for you, Sister Brooks."

"You can just call me Donna."

"It does sound like a promising arrangement," she said and smiled. "Say, since I'm in the area, I'll just stop over during the photo shoot, if you don't mind. That way I'll be on hand if you get into difficulties. I imagine, Sister Brooks ... I mean *Donna*, that you and I will be seeing a lot of each other."

"Could be," said Donna smiling. She knew her contract allowed her access to the church Public Affairs Department, but so far, she hadn't seen the need. Of course, this *was* Sister Monson's business and she probably knew what lay ahead.

"By the way, Sister Monson," asked Donna. "What brings you to our ward?"

"Oh, I like to keep an eye out for where the action is," she responded cheerfully. "And you, Donna, seem to be right in the middle of the action. I wanted to see you myself. I'm sure you know that one can't be too vigilant these days. I deem it my duty and my honor to be there for you."

Donna suddenly felt the need for a Tums and rummaged through her purse for one. Lois stood by smiling. Just then, the dismissal bell rang, and suddenly the foyer was overrun with galloping Primary children. Ben and Nate came up and grabbed and yanked at Donna's skirt.

"Let's get out of here!" Nate shouted.

"Yeah, I'm hungry!" Ben added. "Come on, Mom!"

"Looks like my meter's up," sighed Donna. "Now that you've seen two of my rascals, Lois, are you still sure you want to have lunch with us?"

"Don't forget, I worked at an orangutan preserve," Lois laughed.

"I'll stop over around 1:30 then," said Sister Monson. She headed toward the exit at a brisk clip, smoothing her skirt. At the same time, Stephanie, Simon, and Hank emerged into the boisterous foyer.

Margo, too, whooped a greeting from down the hall. She

waved her arms high in the air over the sea of people. "Oh Donna! I'll be over at your house this afternoon when all the other New York people arrive to make you famous! Don't have any fun until I get there," she yelled louder than any of the Primary kids.

Donna and her entourage left the building. She looked back over her shoulder and saw several women huddled around Margo.

11

The house smelled of the crock pot chili Donna had thrown together in the morning before church. She whipped on an apron and yanked out a box of corn muffin mix. In minutes, the muffins were baking in the oven.

Lois ruffled through her camera bag and brought out some papers. "Hank, I've got a little busy work for you. These are waivers for you to sign for your kids for whatever photos we take today. Do you have a spare hand for a signature?"

"Sure, Lois," said Hank, signing with the pen hanging by the bulletin board.

"Now, what can I do to be helpful?" asked Lois. She stuffed the waivers in her bag.

"How about grabbing some bowls from that cabinet above you," said Hank. "How many are we today, Donna?"

"I guess we're seven with Lois," she said.

"Make that eight, honey!" called Margo as she breezed into the house through the garage door. "I'm glad I made it here before all the lights, camera, and action."

"Hi, Margo," said Donna. "There's not enough action for you around here on a normal Sunday?"

"Very funny," said Margo. "Hey, you're putting the guest of honor to work?"

"You bet," said Hank. "And while we're at it, would you go downstairs and get us some more paper napkins?"

"Slave driver!" Margo laughed.

As she turned toward the stairs, Stephanie rushed up, phone in hand, and nearly ran into her. "Mom, can I go over to Roxanne's? Her guinea pig is about to have babies. Please, Mom?"

"Stephanie, it's Sunday," replied Donna. "You know we stay together as a family on Sundays. That's nothing new."

"Mom, it's the miracle of life!" Stephanie whined.

"You can go over tonight after they've all been safely delivered," Hank said. "Give the poor mama guinea pig some privacy."

"Oh, Dad, you don't understand," Stephanie began. Then with new gusto she added, "Alas, alas, pharisees and hypocrites! Why don't you think about *that* when the camera crew shows up on the *Sabbath*." She disappeared with the phone. Margo emerged triumphantly from the basement with a new package of paper napkins.

"Bowls are out. Anything else I can do?" asked Lois.

"How are you at grating cheese?" Donna asked.

"Great!" laughed Lois.

"*Great*! Did you hear that! Ha, ha!" laughed Margo too loudly. "So, tell me, Lois, who have you been shooting lately besides my best gal pal?" Donna and Hank exchanged looks. Margo was over the top as usual.

"Let's see, Stephanie would like this. I took pictures of the new baby gorilla at the Philadelphia zoo."

"That's a good preparation for shooting Donna!" Margo chortled. Donna snapped her with the dishtowel.

Simon roamed through the kitchen and grabbed some chips out of a bowl, oblivious to everyone. "Take these earphones off and call your brothers and sister for lunch," Hank said, lifting a plug out of Simon's ear.

Eventually everyone gathered at the informal lunch table. Hank said a blessing and began to ladle chili into the bowls. A few minutes later, the doorbell rang. Simon got up to answer it and came back: "It's for you, Mom. Brother Borden and his kids."

She got up and went to the door. Tom Borden had a twin on each leg and Brittany wriggling in his arms. He looked exhausted. "Sister Brooks, I'm so sorry, but it's an emergency. Cindy's not doing well. She's having trouble breathing. She's got this asthma thing and it's kicking in now. We're on the way to the hospital. Could you watch our kids? Sorry to ask this of you, Sister Brooks, but you being her visiting teacher and all ... "

"Of course, Tom, bring them in. No problem," Donna said, taking Brittany from his arms. "Go with Cindy. We'll take care of things here. Take as much time as you need."

"Thanks so much, Sister Brooks," Tom said, rushing to the car.

"Stephanie, Simon!" called Donna. "We have a service opportunity for you!"

"What is it?" asked Stephanie in a moody tone as if it were not obvious with Brittany clinging to Donna's neck and the twins toddling and sniffling.

"What does it pay?" asked Simon.

"You'll get your reward in heaven," said Donna. "Spread out a blanket in the rec room and pour them little bowls of goldfish crackers. Sing some songs. Pretend to go fishing. Put on a video. Come on, you guys, you can handle this. Be imaginative."

"But I'm eating!" said Simon, his mouth full of corn muffin.

"Set up in the rec room," Hank said. "Someone will bring down the rest of your food."

"And watch those kids on the stairs. I doubt the twins can navigate them," called Donna.

"This spoils all my plans," fumed Stephanie, taking Brittany by the hand. Soon the music to *Beauty and the Beast* floated up from the basement.

The doorbell rang again. This time it was Gloria and the camera crew.

"Come on in!" welcomed Donna. "It's bedlam around here."

Gloria walked in, followed by a staff of technicians carrying screens, lights, tripods, and other equipment. "Hi there, Donna. Love the apron!" She leaned toward Donna and blew little air kisses at each cheek. "Smells good in here. Not as good as Sinnamon, but pretty darn good. Lois! Wonderful to see you!"

"Are you hungry? We've got plenty," offered Hank.

"Hi, Hank! Good to see you again!" said Gloria. "We'll pass on the food for now, thanks all the same. Can you show me around the place? I'd like to see which room will be best for our shooting. I love this part. Get to do some directing." Hank and Donna led Gloria, Lois, and the ever curious Margo from room to room.

"What about your basement?" said Gloria. "I doubt we'll need to shoot down there, but it's good to get a read on the personality of the house."

"The rec room, as you can probably tell, is fully occupied at the moment," said Hank. He was leading the way into the noisy play area when the doorbell rang again. Donna opened the door and found Sister Monson smiling in front of her.

"Donna, I'm so glad I can be here for the taping," Sister Monson said. "Have they begun yet?" She peered inside and saw the technicians uncoiling cables and thumping microphones.

"No, my husband is showing Gloria Hewitt from Big Apple around the house. They're in the basement right now. It's chaos down there, I'm sure. We've had three unexpected kids show up—kids of someone I visit teach."

"Well, good," said Sister Monson. "This gives us a moment to meet privately."

"Fine," said Donna cheerfully.

"Is there a quiet place?" Sister Monson asked.

An odd request, Donna thought, but she was feeling agreeable. "We can go on up to my bedroom if you want," she volunteered.

"That would be lovely."

When they got into the bedroom, Sister Monson dropped to her knees in front of Donna's closet and assumed a prayerful posture. Donna followed suit. "Our dearest eternal ... " began Sister Monson. Her words twined and blossomed over her outline of topics. "We are gathered today at the launching of this offering to thy kingdom, this witness to the world of thy will for the lives of all those who love and serve you ... "

This seemed odd to Donna. It was just perfume, for heavens sake, not a fatted calf. But then, what did she know about public affairs? Donna tried to remain reverent, but every so often she heard loud thumps from the basement followed by either peals of laughter or agonized wailing, she couldn't make out which.

"Guide and protect our dear Sister Donna Brooks and her loved ones as they embark ..."

You'd think we were setting off on the *Titanic*, Donna thought.

"Quicken her wisdom, her abilities, improve and strengthen her physical sense of self. Grant her an introduction to thy Spirit and its mysterious ways ..."

Wait a minute, thought Donna. I appreciate all the help I can get, but with this new haircut and color and the whole crew of folks, including Rico, I am no longer chopped liver, thank you very much. And an "introduction to thy Spirit?" It seems to me the Spirit and I are already on speaking terms. Aren't Cindy Borden's kids in my basement at this very moment?

"Keep her from pride, from greed, from lust, from all manner of sins as she traffics in the ways of the world." Sister Monson's voice was dulcet, but Donna caught the sharp barbs.

At that instant, Donna heard the doorbell ring again. "Sorry to interrupt, Sister Monson," she said, and then got awkwardly up

69

off her knees. "The doorbell rang and I'm sure the rest of the family can't hear it."

Sister Monson opened her eyes, gave a slight sneer, closed her eyes again for a quick wrap up amen, and then stood up.

The doorbell rang again. It had just rung a third time when Donna opened it. There stood Roxanne holding a guinea pig crate in a large cardboard box.

"Hi, Mrs. Brooks?" Roxanne said. "Stephanie said to bring Gwyneth over? She's in labor? Not much time left? See? Isn't this great?"

Donna looked into the wire cage and saw poor Gwyneth wincing and heaving her furry bulky body. "Good heavens, Roxanne. Here comes one now!"

"Oh, is this cool or what?" shrieked Roxanne. Poor Gwyneth just panted and squeezed.

"Come on in, Roxanne. Set her down over there." Donna went to the rec room door and called to Stephanie: "Gwyneth is having babies. Come up right now and see!" Everyone came bolting up from the basement, kids and adults and even a camera man.

"Get all the cameras rolling, guys!" yelled Gloria. "How much homier can we get? Hey, Donna, why don't you get over there by Gwyneth and act as midwife or something."

"She's not even my guinea pig!" Donna protested.

Gloria was beyond hearing. She was busy orchestrating all the cameramen.

"Besides, she's doing fine all by herself," Donna added. "See, here comes number two!"

"She did number two in the cage? Gross!" yelled Ben.

The larger kids crowded around the cage. The smaller ones, eager to see what the excitement was about, yanked and pounded, trying to get through.

"Not *that* number two," said Simon, rubbing his knuckles on Ben's head. "She's having babies."

"And it's gross!" groaned Nate.

"I want to see gross!" Ben yelled, trying to pry his way to the cage. "I want to see gross!"

"It truly is the miracle of life," said Stephanie. The words came out unsteady and insincere. She seemed a little pale watching the proceedings in living color.

Donna looked up to hear a technician cursing as one of the twins wandered off and plucked the duct tape off a cable and was starting to twist it around. "I'll take him off your hands," said Donna, snatching up the renegade. She looked up for a moment to see Sister Monson on the landing of the stairs heading from the bedroom. She was once again in prayer mode but not kneeling this time, thankfully, although still with eyes shut and hands folded reverently, her lips moving.

"We're up to three!" shouted Margo, peering in above the heads of the children.

Lois moved around the room clicking her camera from all angles. Donna marveled at her agility to squat down, then spring up, to wedge herself into tiny spots for just the right angle.

Little Brittany Borden ambled over toward Donna and tugged at her apron. Hank came over, the other twin in his arm, and gave Donna a squeeze around the waist. Ben and Nate ran over and took cover next to Hank while Simon grabbed bark from the cage and threatened to toss it at them.

"Stop that right now, Simon!" shouted Donna. "Give that poor animal some rest. Keep your hands out of that cage. I wouldn't blame her if she bit you."

Stephanie came over and leaned her head wearily on Donna's shoulder. "Childbirth is exhausting," she sighed. Whichever twin Donna was holding started patting Stephanie's head affectionately.

"Hey, lady," Hank said to Donna, "you've got some chili on your neck. Let me take care of that for you." He tried to wipe it off with his finger, but the smudge would not come off. He leaned over and kissed it clean. "Delicious!" he hummed.

"Baby number 4!" Margo announced.

Simon came over, stalking Ben. When Donna warned him, he held up his empty hands to show his innocence. The twin Hank was holding grabbed Simon and hugged him ferociously around the neck.

Roxanne and Margo kept vigil on the birthing, the squealing family now totaling five babies and one beleaguered mom.

"And ... cut!" yelled Gloria. "That's a wrap! Fantastic, Donna! This is so fabulous. I couldn't have asked for better. We have miles of workable footage here."

"What do you mean, it's a wrap?" said Sister Monson from the stair landing.

"Who are you?" asked Gloria.

"I'm Meredith Monson, Public Affairs, The Church of Jesus Christ of Latter-day Saints," came the dreamy voice. She produced a business card in the palm of her hand, like magic, and handed it across the melee to Gloria.

"Oh, I see," said Gloria, warily. "You're the one who provided the lawyer?"

"Yes."

"And you're here today exactly why?" Gloria asked.

"Draw in your talons, Gloria," Lois said quietly. "I met her earlier. She's someone from Donna's church and here to help Donna. If her day is usually like this, that's a pretty nice service to provide, don't you think?" Her goodwill managed to soothe things.

"Fine, fine, whatever," Gloria said. "We're done, I think. I'll be in touch about when we'll need you in New York next. We've got this raw material to process and package up for the print ads and other assignments to line up. We've got to hit our timing just right for the holiday season. If we trot you out too soon, you'll be old news by the time St. Nick comes to town. There's a science to this. But you can just relax for a couple of weeks."

"Wait a minute. You say you're done?" Donna said. "But I haven't had a chance to answer any questions or talk about how I made the product—show you where it all began. All of that."

"If we need more, I'm sure we'll be back. For now, this little serendipity was just great!"

"Besides, Mom," Simon volunteered. "They asked us all kinds of questions in the basement. They know all about you; don't worry."

12

Donna spent the next three weeks in pleasant normalcy. General Conference came and went. Over Columbus Day weekend, they trekked off to the Berkshires for a little hiking. Assuming that the end of the month was going to get crazy, Donna got out the Halloween costumes. Life was just what she was used to—chauffeuring, picking up messes, shopping, the occasional soap opera with lunch.

Even Margo's promotional zeal cooled when day after day came and went with no reports. Donna was starting to worry that it had all been some kind of peri-menopausal fantasy. But one morning she knew it was no fantasy.

"Did you see it yet?"

"See what?" croaked Donna groggily into the receiver. The clock by her bedside read 6:30 a.m.

"The ad!" Margo said. "The ad in the *Globe*! It's an insert—like those sample boxes of cereal or Advil or winged pads or whatever. It's terrific! Go check it out and call me later!"

Donna wrapped her robe around her, shuffled out of the house in her slippers, and picked up the paper. The glossy insert slipped out. There it was: "Sinnamon: A scent you can't forget; a scent that makes you remember." There was a full-color photo of Hank kissing Donna. The kiss was splendid, in crisp focus and full of promise, Donna's eyes dreamily half shut, and Hank looking ardent and intent, nuzzling her neck.

In black and white, in a fuzzier, softer light, was a baby at Donna's shoulder, another child in front of her, some girl leaning against her, and another youngster in Hank's arms. The Borden's twins! Stephanie! Ben! She barely remembered. That was the kiss to get the chili off her neck! Transformed by camera wizardry, it looked like a blissful, romantic moment in the middle of daily pandemonium. Superimposed on the photo were the words: "In the busyness of life, it is easy to lose sight of its loveliness." Framing the photo were the repeated words in elegant calligraphy—"Oh yes, Sinnamon. Yes."

Best of all, there was a little scratch-and-sniff patch that gave a whiff of Sinnamon. "Buy it at fine cosmetics counters beginning Monday at noon." This wasn't cheesy or salacious. This was tasteful, provocative, and still wholesome.

Wait a minute, Donna thought. I was supposed to have artistic input. Here this comes without my knowing a thing about it? Well, maybe there was something in those waivers for the photographs, some fine print she should have read. Besides, what did it matter? The ad was terrific! Donna loved it!

Apparently the rest of the city loved it, too. Donna's phone began ringing. By noon, she finally quit answering and let the machine pick up. Hank called at 2:00 from work. He called, hung up after one ring, and then called back—their signal—to report on his new studly reputation at work.

Driving into town to pick up the dry cleaning that afternoon, Donna saw lines of people outside Filene's. In front of the store was a huge marquee with a reproduction of the photo and a handwritten label diagonally across the photo that read: "Hometown inventor: Donna Brooks!" Some people in line recognized her in the minivan and started chanting and pointing like merry little groupies.

"Could you sign right here, Mrs. Brooks?" asked the dry cleaner when she picked up Hank's suits.

"Sure. But you know, I've been coming in here for years. Is this some new policy?"

The dry cleaner laughed, holding her delicate hand to her mouth. "Oh, no, Mrs. Brooks! Oh no! It's your autograph I want! I love Sinnamon! I sent my son over to Filene's to stand in line for me. He got me ten vials. I'm so proud to know you, and my aunt in Toronto told me to get your autograph, too."

"Toronto?" Donna said.

"The ad is in all the papers, even in Canada. Didn't you know? I e-mailed my sister in Honolulu," she continued, "and she told me to stock up and send her some to sell on the secondary market. She made a fortune off Beanie Babies that way."

Donna walked out in a daze and had to turn around half way down the block when she remembered her suits were still hanging on the hook inside the cleaners. When she got home, there were sixty-four messages on the machine.

"This is crazy!" Donna said, giggling to herself. She looked at the ad in the paper again and longed to have Hank home. After school, the kids came roaring through the door, slamming it behind them.

"What's the deal?" Donna asked.

"There's a crowd of girls after Simon and Nate and a crowd of boys after Stephanie!" laughed Ben.

"Everybody had their scratch and sniffs with them at school today," said Simon. "Fame is terrific. They got this new chant going in the cafeteria: 'Oh yes, Simon, yes!' It's a riot! I am so popular!"

"Yeah," agreed Nate. "Everybody was giving me the best stuff out of their lunches."

"Me too, Mom," added Ben. "My teacher Miss Erickson

wants you to come in and talk to the class for career day. Can you do that? I told her it was okay but that you didn't really have a career. You just stay at home and do nothing."

After everyone was settled with snacks and after-school activities, Donna sat down to listen to the phone messages. Of the sixty-four, ten were from Margo wanting to know "all the details."

Ten messages were from Gloria: one saying she had lined up a *Good Morning America* taping for Wednesday, one to say she had arranged a mall appearance in New Jersey on Thursday, and another saying she was working on *Live with Regis & Kelly* and David Letterman. She wanted to know if Donna didn't think the ad in the paper was fabulous. And how was the response at home? "Get yourself a beeper," she continued, "and I'll reimburse you because it's getting annoying having to leave messages." "Buy a fax, too," she said, because how would she relay the plane schedule? Mrs. Monson from Donna's church called "to congratulate us on the ad." Did Donna really invite this woman to be present at all the TV tapings? Gloria wanted to know. Because she's saying she'll be there on Wednesday for *GMA*. The first statistics from Lucy show they've sold out in eight of ten New York stores carrying Sinnamon. Be sure to watch *Entertainment Tonight* at 8:00, Gloria added, to see what they did with the video segment.

Other messages were from ward members and neighbors wishing Donna well and congratulating "Hank, you old fox," for "looking so sexy." Ten were from lawyers offering their assistance in protecting Donna's interests with her new product. One was from Tom Borden asking her to call him back at home. One was from Lois trying to set a convenient time for the Vineyard trip, and could the whole family come? One was from Juliet saying she'd heard from Lois and looked forward to the trip, possibly this weekend? Another from Juliet wondered when they would go visiting teaching? She had tried but hadn't reached Margo. Any suggestions? There was also a message from Hank saying he loved her.

Which to respond to first? Donna wondered. Simple. She dialed Hank's number. His voice mail picked up. "I love you, too, you handsome hunk," she said. "Can't wait to see you."

Then she called Tom Borden. "Hi, Tom. I know we didn't have much time to talk when you came by for the kids the other night. How's Cindy doing?"

"She's doing okay. When we went to the hospital, they gave her a new medicine and a fancy kind of inhaler. The doctor says it gets worse with stress, but I can't figure out why she's stressed. I mean, her life is just what she always wanted—a husband and lots of kids. She's pregnant again. Isn't that great? Anyway, I know she misses her mom and all, but we'll see her at Christmas time and for a week over the summer. She keeps crying, which makes it harder for her to breathe. Anyway, the reason I called is we've been getting calls all day from parents at Brittany's pre-school saying they saw Ammon and Brigham in a newspaper ad today. My mom in Pocatello saw it too. A neighbor brought the picture over and it really is them. I don't get it. When did you have a picture taken of them?"

Donna sat silent for a long while.

"Sister Brooks, are you still there?" Tom asked.

"Yes, Tom," Donna said. "I'm trying to understand how this all happened myself. Back in late September, we had some photographers here at the house. They had us sign waivers for the kids. Only our kids were here at the time. You arrived with your little guys right after that. We just expected our kids to be in the shots. I'm afraid I didn't read the waivers that carefully. It was a little wild here, as you can imagine. Then this morning the ad shows up, and I didn't even remember that that photo was taken. It took me a while to recognize who everybody was. I'm sorry, Tom."

"Oh, I understand, I guess," said Tom vaguely. "But the stuff

77

does smell good. Good luck with it, Sister Brooks. Well, I can hear Cindy's asthma acting up. She's been saying crazy things today like maybe you'd make a better mother since you're so close to the Spirit and because the boys look so happy in the picture and everything. Then she carries on about whether it's okay to treat her asthma on Sunday. She's so weepy all the time, I can't quite figure it out. Maybe it's one of those pregnancy emotions, do you think? Anyhow, Sister Brooks, I think that maybe you shouldn't use our kids again."

"No, Tom, of course not. Can I try to make it up to you some way? Can I at least bring you some meals?"

"Food? Yeah, we could use some food," said Tom. "Although Cindy doesn't keep much down."

"How about babysitting? My daughter Stephanie is fourteen. She could come over after school tomorrow and give you guys a break." Donna didn't like volunteering Stephanie without checking with her, but a couple of casseroles seemed so lame.

"I do have to take Cindy back for a check-up with the doctor tomorrow afternoon," Tom said. "It would help us a lot if we didn't have to have the kids with us."

"What time do you want her there?" Donna asked.

"Is 3:30 okay?" Tom asked.

"Perfect," Donna said. "Stephanie gets home around 3:00, so I'll have her to you by 3:30."

The next call was to Margo.

"You are an official celebrity now!" said Margo.

Donna told her about the messages from Gloria about Letterman, *Good Morning America*, *Regis and Kelly*, about the *Entertainment Tonight* segment.

"Hey, maybe I'll show up in that last one! I've got to make sure the VCR is working." Donna wished she could match Margo's enthusiasm for the upcoming TV interviews, but she felt bad about Cindy and Tom Borden. She mentioned it to Margo.

"There's an easy solution," Margo said lightly. "Tom is a new hire and he's still a graduate student. They're poor as church mice. The biggest help would be obvious. Forget the hot casseroles; how 'bout some cold, hard cash? You're going to have plenty of it soon. Just give some of it to Tom and Lizzy Borden."

"Lizzy Borden? It's *Cindy* Borden," Donna corrected.

"Whatever," Margo said nonchalantly. "Set up a scholarship fund or something. How guilty do you feel, anyway? It's not as if you *intended* to use their kids."

Margo had a way of making compassionate service sound so brutal. Although Margo had a point, Donna would have to think on it. "Hey, Margo," she said, changing subjects. "Juliet tells me she's been trying to reach you to set up a visiting teaching appointment."

"Yeah, I hear the messages, but I'm always gabbing away with you, so doesn't that count?" Margo said. "Besides, that woman rubs me the wrong way. I can't put my finger on it. It just always feel like she's judging me."

"I've never gotten that feeling from her. In fact, I don't think she's judgmental at all."

"Well, you two have obviously bonded." Margo said.

"If you'd ever let us come and visit you, you might find you like her," Donna said.

"And when, Miss Entertainment Tonight, am I going to squeeze myself into your schedule?" She laughed.

"Well, I'm supposed to be done with this next batch on Sunday sometime. Oh, but then I'm going to Martha's Vineyard, I think."

"What's this?" asked Margo. "Martha's Vineyard? How did you manage a sweet little get-away like that? Is there room for me? Leave Hank at home, I'd be better company."

"Lois Wheaton, you know, the photographer, invited us out for the weekend, along with Juliet Benton."

There was a pause. "With Juliet?" Margo asked incredulously.

79

"Oh, don't take it personally," Donna teased. "Lois knows Juliet. She's known her since she was a teenager. It'll be 'old home week' for them. I'll probably be stuck on shore yanking sea urchin spines out of my feet."

"Yeah, right," said Margo. "You and the brain will be out there with the rich and famous, dining at the Black Dog on Big Apple's expense account."

Donna laughed. "Lighten up, Margo."

"I'm just going to go get my cross-stitching out right now and start working on the pillow I want to give you for Christmas," Margo said. "It'll be something in green and red, maybe with a sachet in the middle—a cinnamon sachet—and it'll say: 'Margo knew me when ...' But hey, I need to set up the VCR to record *Entertainment Tonight*. Call me when you get back in town. Bring me some of the goodies they give you—from Regis or whatever. How about Letterman's autograph, or is that tacky?"

"I'll see what I can do. No promises," said Donna, "until you let Juliet and me come by and visit teach."

"Oh, Donna. I need to go buy a bigger dictionary so I can get through a conversation with her. Hey, I really do need to get to the VCR. Bye now!"

Donna went straight to the kitchen and pulled out her favorite cookbook and put the sauce pan on the stove top. She wanted to get started on the casserole for the Bordens while she was still thinking about it. She had a tasty rigatoni recipe that was simple to whip up and would make enough for them and Donna's family. She turned on a CD. Before she forgot, she called upstairs to Stephanie about the babysitting arrangements.

She expected moaning from Stephanie. Instead, Stephanie said, "That'll be fine. I don't have rehearsals tomorrow and I kind of like Brittany. Roxanne named three of the guinea pig babies Brigham, Ammon, and Brittany."

That triggered another wave of guilt. Donna stirred the bubbling pot of tomato sauce and spices and tried to focus on how to make things better. All the while, the Dixie Chicks kept up a lively tempo on the CD. Donna boogied and stirred cheerfully. Noodles boiled to just the right tenderness. Ground beef turned from pink to brown and cheese melted smoothly. Lettuce tossed up pertly into two bowls with chopped cucumber, cherry tomatoes, and a boiled egg, all arranged in a star pattern. The salad for the Bordens would chill in the refrigerator. The timer dinged. Two pans of rigatoni emerged from the oven smelling good enough for Wolfgang Puck.

Donna replaced the Dixie Chicks with Yo Yo Ma cello solos for *tafelmusik*. "Chow time!" she called downstairs and up, just as Hank walked in the door. Perfect timing. Nate blessed the food, and they had a lovely meal. No squabbles, no embarrassments, no spills. During their meal, fifty million TV viewers across the nation learned what enquiring minds wanted to know about the "Secret Life of Sinnamon."

13

At 8:31 p.m. the phone rang again. Donna had developed the habit of not answering, but Stephanie *always* answered. "Mom! Phone's for you. It's Sister Monson," called Stephanie. She let the receiver clank against the wall.

Donna got a portable phone from the study and hung up the kitchen phone. "Hi, Sister Monson. I understand you're planning to be at the taping for *Good Morning America* on Wednesday," said Donna lightly.

"Yes, yes, we'll get to that. But Sister Brooks, we have to talk about tonight's show," said Sister Monson urgently.

"What do you mean, 'tonight's show'?" asked Donna.

"The *Entertainment Tonight* broadcast just now. Didn't you see it?"

"Oh, for goodness sake! I forgot all about it!" Donna said, a rush of embarrassment heating her face. "How was it?"

"Let's just say we have some repair work to do," Sister Monson said.

"What do you mean?" Donna asked.

"It's going to be hard to talk about it if you haven't seen it. I thought you would have watched it. Sister Brooks, you have a stewardship here," her voice turned chill, "and you've got to pay more attention. A lot is at stake, and we really don't like to do damage control if we can help it."

"You're right that I'm at a disadvantage not having seen the tape," said Donna. She would give an inch in the apology department, but not a mile. "I was having a pleasant meal with the family," Donna said, then quickly added, "being Monday night, after all. We were just about to settle in for a little family night when the phone rang."

"The ox is in the mire, Sister Brooks."

Something occurred to Donna. "Just a minute, Sister Monson," she said. "My friend was going to make a tape. I'll get her copy, watch it, and then talk to you after that. How about you call back in an hour?" Donna hung up and called Margo.

Margo appeared five minutes later with her tape. "Your premiere! Donna, you're going to love it. It's terrific!" she gushed.

"That's not what Sister Monson seemed to think," Donna said.

"She needs to loosen up. Come on, everyone!" sang Margo. "It's time to see yourselves on TV!"

Everyone collected in front of the rec room TV as the opening credits rolled. They chuckled through segments on celebrity marriages and celebrity tattoos and Disney's next animated movie. Then came the part they were waiting for: "The Secret Life of Sinnamon." They stared wide-eyed for a moment and then, well, to say they laughed would be an understatement. If laughter were helium, then the entire house would have up and hied to Kolob. They could not stop laughing.

"My favorite part was when Simon belched in your face and Stephanie said, 'Smells like Sinnamon to me!'" laughed Nate.

"I liked the part when Stephanie said, 'Our mother's especially good at making children,' and then Ammon and Brigham and Brittany jumped out and did peek-a-boo," said Simon. "They didn't show the part where we said that Mom is good at drawing."

"And when they asked Ben what he liked to do on the weekends," laughed Stephanie, "and he said, 'Make spit wads and see how close I can get to hitting the bishop at church.'"

"I thought it was a hoot when Margo kept calling everybody 'honey'—even Dad!" laughed Donna.

"And then Nate piped up with, 'She's always over here. She's like a second mom to us.' Boy, am I going to get razzed at work tomorrow!" laughed Hank.

"And that part when Stephanie told how she and Mom gave each other tattoos" Simon roared.

"But not that they were those goofy wash-off kind from the Easter egg kits!" Donna wheezed, holding her side.

"What a surprise when Stephanie lifted her sleeve to show that little bunny!" gasped Hank. They rewound to that section and played it a few more times, although they couldn't hear it over all the hardy-har-harring. Exhausted, they finally went upstairs and made root beer floats.

"Looks like we had Family Home Evening after all!" sighed Donna.

"So what's Sister Monson in such a snit about?" asked Margo. "I thought that was great."

"I suppose a few places could have used a little smoothing over, *honey!*" teased Donna.

"Oh yeah, well, that," giggled Margo. "But for my fifteen seconds of fame, that's a nice way to get it."

"I think it's fifteen *minutes*," Donna corrected.

"For you it was minutes, for me it was a few seconds." Margo said.

"I really thought I was supposed to be able to see promotional material before they released it. I'd better ask about that," Donna said. "But this was fun anyway. I'm starting to trust their judgment. At least, nobody's wearing black leather in those posters."

"More's the pity," laughed Margo. "I suppose Sister Monson is going to be calling now. I'm surprised the phone hasn't already rung."

"After I called you, I put it on pick-up," Donna said. "I'd better see if she called." She had. Several times. As soon as Donna put the phone back on regular ring, Sister Monson called again. "Hi, Sister Monson," Donna said.

Margo scribbled "I'm going to listen in on the portable" on a post-it note and skulked off to eavesdrop.

"Sister Brooks, I assume you've seen the portion now?" Sister Monson began.

"Yes, and frankly, I don't understand what your complaint is," Donna said evenly. "Our family thought it was hilarious."

"Hilarious?" said Sister Monson, her voice icy again.

"We thought it was a great—a little light-hearted romp with the family—a real family that's fun-loving and, okay, a bit quirky and has a goofy sense of humor. But it captured us pretty well, we decided. We gave it a thumbs up."

There was silence on the other end. Margo grinned and gave Donna a thumbs up of her own. "Sister Brooks. Perhaps it is because public affairs is not your field, but you have clearly failed to see the repercussions of this kind of folderol. This 'light-hearted romp' as you call it has already resulted in several calls from Salt Lake."

Margo scribbled "Probably all from her relatives" on another post-it.

84

"They're very touchy out there about polygamy," continued Sister Monson.

"Polygamy? Oh, for goodness sake," laughed Donna. "Nobody could seriously read *that* into it! It was just a joke!"

"Maybe where *you* live, but not out there, let me assure you!" said Sister Monson. "And beyond that, your children's lack of proper regard for authority. That's an issue we have to nip in the bud. We can't have children being surly and disrespectful. Haven't they read the pamphlets on youth standards? Spit wads thrown at church leaders? Sister Brooks, it's got to be nipped."

Now the silence was on Donna's end of the line. The lioness was starting to throb. "I've got to go now, Sister Monson," she said, her voice as controlled as she could make it.

"Yes, I imagine you have your work cut out for you tonight," said Sister Monson, her voice creamy again, assuming victory. "I look forward to seeing you on Wednesday in New York. We can go over a few more items before your taping." Click.

"You are a model of self-control!" said Margo. "I would have shredded her. The nerve! Who does she think she is?"

"She is 'Sister Monson, stake Public Affairs director.' Maybe she knows something about public affairs," Donna added, "but she can keep her mitts off my private affairs and stop picking on my kids!"

"That's right, honey! Although they're not so private anymore, not after tonight," Margo added. "Hey, that was Sister Monson at your house that night, right? Is that *Meredith* Monson?"

"Yeah, I think so," said Donna. "Why? Have you heard of her?"

"My daughter at U. Mass said a Meredith Monson made quite a name for herself with some company that does cleaning products through radio ads and home sales. Really high up in the ranks. Supposed to be a real success. She's done a lot of voice-overs for their commercials for cleaning solvents. What a voice! It's mesmerizing! I hosted a party for that stuff after hearing her.

Other than that, I don't think she's got any experience with public affairs unless getting stains out of rugs counts. She has some big clients, though—corporations that use the stuff and management types.

"But here's the thing," continued Margo. "She was called to be a nursery assistant in the Amherst Ward, but it didn't last a month, so Michelle tells me. That's something, isn't it? How often do you hear about nursery assistants getting released after a few weeks?"

"That's probably not all that uncommon," said Donna. "Not everyone's cut out for it."

"Especially not people who think that toddlers should act like recruits," said Margo. "From what Michelle told me, she had them marching around with their arms folded like little Hitler youth."

"There's a grim picture for you!" said Donna. "I'm sure she means well and everything. I don't have anything against her." Then her voice tightened: "But still, I don't care how many voice-over commercials she's made or how many gallons of cleanser she's sold or how many lawyers and CEO's jump when she snaps her fingers. *She'd better not criticize my kids!*"

"Amen, sister!" cheered Margo.

"What do you think?" asked Donna. "If this Sinnamon stuff really ends up being a big deal ..."

"Honey, it already is!" said Margo.

"Okay, then. What about that 'every member a missionary' thing? Is Sinnamon my product or, because I'm Mormon, am I supposed to be marketing the gospel along with it? If I decide to 'let my light so shine' and all that, do I have to screw in the public-image light bulb that Sister Monson wants? The one that says we don't throw spit wads at bishops or get tattoos? Or is it my own kind of bulb that laughs and likes to think that God might be laughing along with me?"

"This brings us to the more important question," said

Margo: "How many Mormons does it take to change a light bulb?"

"Oh, Margo! Alright, how many Mormons does it take to change a light bulb?"

"Five—one to change the bulb and four to bring refreshments!" She laughed.

"Isn't that the truth!" Donna laughed, too.

That night, Donna had troubled dreams. She saw herself teetering on a ladder high inside the Tabernacle on Temple Square trying to change the light bulbs. That morphed into a picture of her standing at the podium at her local ward while the congregation threw spit wads at her. Then she was on a tight rope, Margo wriggling on her shoulders. Rico, the wardrobe guy, held one end of the rope and Sister Monson held the other. Suddenly she was on Martha's Vineyard trying to ride a bicycle along the coast, but the pedals moved in slow motion. Everywhere she looked along the shore, there were cows hip-deep in mud and muck. They bellowed out to her in low, anxious voices, "Donna, save us! Donna, save us!"

When Donna arrived at the ABC studios on Wednesday, Gloria and an ABC host gave her a quick tour of the facilities. "You'll be fine with the taping!" cheered Gloria. "I think they've got Elizabeth Vargas on for the interview. She's a doll. She'll put you right at ease. She always does. Well, guess it's time for you to get made up. You'll be with Philip today. Maddy doesn't do the *Good Morning America* shoots," said Gloria. I'll catch up with you afterwards. Good luck!"

"Yes, Mrs. Brooks," said Philip, the make-up artist. "You look great! Don't think we'll have to do much. Just enough to keep the glare off your forehead. I'm sure you know the drill." After such a short time, Donna surprisingly already did know the drill.

Philip proved to be a chatterbox. "Just love your Sinnamon,

Mrs. Brooks! I gave some to my girlfriend and I think that cinched the deal! We're getting married next month!"

"Congratulations, Philip!" Donna said. "That's wonderful!"

"Couldn't have done it without you." He regaled her with the story of his first date with his new fiancee and began launching into his Internet explorations of honeymoon sites when the door opened.

"At last I've found you!" sighed Sister Monson, triumphantly.

"I love it when people say that to me! Hi there," said Philip cheerfully. "Can we help you with something?"

"I'm here to coach you for your interview," she said to Donna, completely ignoring Philip. It was hard to ignore Philip, a black, bald-headed, six-foot-three, 280-pound make-up artist in the tiny room they were squeezed into. "I got caught up in traffic and I'm awfully late," said Sister Monson to Donna only. "Thankfully, I made it here before your taping, so there's no damage done."

"Okey-dokey," said Philip agreeably. "Just pretend I'm not here and go at it, ladies."

"Time is of the essence," Sister Monson continued unruffled. "You have only so much time to make some important points. First, family values. Proclaim it as traditionally as possible. You've got some misunderstandings to clear up from the other night! This would be the time to mention the delight of reverent children, how you emphasize obedience and respect in the family. I'll send you some pamphlets for remedial assistance in that. Of course, you can bring up the degrading effects of raucous laughter and body mutilations.

"You're not just selling hearth and home, Sister Brooks. You're selling heaven, if you think about it. It's a blessing and a weighty responsibility you're under!" Sister Monson took a deep breath. She was not yet done.

"Where was I? Oh, two—no mention of s-e-x. Nothing suggestive in the slightest! Pretend you don't understand the concept.

"Three, call it 'The Church of Jesus Christ,' fortissimo, then add on the 'of Latter-day Saints' part but quieter. Don't call it Mormonism. Yes, I know it's a little long, but it's good to get it out there over the airwaves.

"Four, if you can mention the missionaries, all the better. Don't mention that you're using the money from Sinnamon to finance your children's missions, though. The public just won't be ready yet for that. Believe me, I've learned that lesson from my own marketing experience.

"By the way, that reminds me that I've got some cleaner I'm going to send you for those stains on your rec room carpet. Remind me to send you a sample.

"Now let's see, what else," she rushed on. She held up her fingers and counted off. "Family values, no s-e-x, name of church, missionaries. Hmmm. I thought of something else last night. Oh yes, just be yourself—your better self. We want you to appear as wholesome and pure as a sweet fragrance in the nostrils of God."

At that, Sister Monson inhaled deeply, exhaled, and stood up. "That should cover it. Good luck." She snapped the door behind her.

Donna longed to have something break the awkwardness she felt. She wanted to hear Philip's Internet discoveries. Anything. Philip just brushed some blush on her face and whispered, "Lord have mercy."

14

Donna agreed with Gloria. Elizabeth Vargas was a doll. So friendly and warm, relaxed, and unbelievably pretty with her petite brunette look. In fact, she could easily be intimidating to someone like Donna who constantly fretted over her middle-aged pouch. But Elizabeth was delightful, and whatever anxieties Sister Monson stirred up slipped smoothly away. Donna could not remember what Sister Monson's admonitions had been, they were so scattergun and breathless. Donna remembered something about the stains in her rec room carpet needing cleaning, but that couldn't be something to emphasize, could it?

The interview covered areas that were easy to talk about. How had she come to make Sinnamon in the first place? "Just a little party favor for the ladies at church" she replied. What did her family think of the product. "The kids like it. My husband likes it. Even the elderly folks at church seem to like it quite a bit." How would you describe the smell, recognizing that it's tricky to describe a smell on television. "I wanted to capture something of all those good, familiar things like comfort and love and nourishment and mix it up with a little bit of pizzazz. I think I succeeded."

Gloria met her after the interview. "You were fabulous!" she gushed. "You were relaxed. You were matter-of-fact but not arrogant. I loved the line, 'I think I succeeded.' Great bit. Couldn't have scripted it better myself. Loved the homey touch about the ladies at church. And *sooooo* glad you mentioned the pizzazz thing. Can't forget that. You're a pro, Donna. A pro! Tomorrow I've got a Cherry Hill mall promotional lined up at noon. It'll seem like small potatoes after this, but it's part of marketing, dear. On Friday the *GMA* interview will air, and that night, we've got you lined up for the new Broadway musical *Whiff and Poof*."

"Really? *Whiff and Poof*? I heard a review of that. It's supposed to be great! Do you think Hank could come?" Donna asked.

"Sure, sure, but we're not done yet! Saturday we have taping sessions for a commercial and then Sunday morning a brunch at the Plaza. We'll have you winging your way back to Boston by 2:00. Sound like enough to keep you out of mischief?"

That evening from her hotel room, Donna called Hank. "The interview went really well, and you should hear the events they've got me scheduled for. I'm exhausted just thinking about it. Hank, can you come down on Friday? I'm supposed to be at a Broadway play. How about joining me for that?"

"Donna, that's Ben and Nate's parents' night at school," Hank said.

"You're kidding? They scheduled it for a Friday night and they're not letting us know until now?" Donna groaned.

"It's been on the school calendar. We just never checked," Hank said. "Sorry, sweetheart. I'd love to be there with you, but I think one of us needs to be here for the boys. As it is, it'll be tricky to spread myself between both boys' schedules."

"Do you think I should come back?" Donna asked.

"No, we're fine!" Hank said. "I really do like this cooking thing. Tonight we're having french toast and bacon for supper. I told the kids to pretend we're in France having breakfast instead of in Boston having dinner."

Donna could hear the kids singing "Frere Jacques" in the background. She felt hollow inside. "I miss you, Hank. I miss the kids. I can't believe you actually got them singing!" she sighed.

"You should see Stephanie! She put on a beret and drew a little black moustache with an eyebrow pencil," Hank said.

Stephanie wearing a beret? Acting whimsical? Was this her daughter?

"Don't worry about us, Donna," Hank reassured her. "We're doing great! We're all having a ball. You should, too. Go on and enjoy the play. Bring the program home and tell me all about it when you get back on Sunday."

"But we're going to Martha's Vineyard on Sunday, remember?" Donna said.

"What?" Hank asked.

"To Lois Wheaton's place when I get back. You and the kids, Juliet Benton, too—you know, my visiting teaching companion."

"This is the first I've heard about it, honey. It sounds great, but I've got that high council assignment in Foxboro. The stake president would club me if I ditched it," Hank said.

"Oh, no, I can't believe I forgot to tell you!" groaned Donna. "Everything's just been moving too fast. I really wanted to go."

"You *can* go. The kids can go, too. It's just that *I* can't go," Hank said.

"But I miss you," Donna said gloomily. She could feel her eyes starting to fill.

"Is this an overnighter?" Hank asked.

"Yeah, just over Sunday, then back on Monday. I think it's a teacher training day Monday, so the kids won't have school."

"Do the kids know about this? I mean, since you didn't tell me, did you tell them?"

Donna tried to remember. "I told Margo. I think I told the kids, but I can't remember," said Donna.

She heard Hank's voice yelling muffled questions to the kids. "They haven't heard about it either, but they're happy to come if we can make it work," Hank said. "It looks like I won't see you until Monday night then."

"I guess that's right," Donna said. "I miss you, Hank."

"Miss you, too, honey! Gotta go now. There was just a thud upstairs in Ben's room that I'd better go check. Love you! Call me!" Donna put down the phone, crawled into bed and fell into a melancholy slumber.

The next day's trip to the mall was a blur. Donna wanted to slip out and get Simon a backpack she saw advertised on sale, but with the camera men and the make-up people and the whole entourage, she couldn't get loose. She managed to escape to the ladies room, but when she got out of the stall, there was a line of women waiting outside to get her autograph. "Would you sign this paper towel for me?" said one fawning young woman. "I don't know who you are, but you must be someone important."

After the *GMA* interview aired, the phone started ringing in

Donna's hotel room. Gloria warned her this might happen and told her to refer calls to her. "Ms. Brooks, Roger Reed here from *USA Today*," barked an eager voice. "Tell me about the Sinnamon phenomenon!" "Love your product, Miss Brooks," said another. "How did you come up with the idea?" "Ms. Brooks, you've brought warmth and excitement to the country. How about bringing some to me—Park Plaza, room 512. I'll be waiting."

After that one, Donna quit answering the phone at all. A reporter showed up disguised as a housekeeper, so she hung the Do Not Disturb sign on the door and collapsed onto the bed. She imagined her kids playing happily without her, her husband cooking cheerfully without her, life going on merrily without her.

At 6:00 p.m. she woke up to more knocking on the door. "Open up, doll! It's me, Gloria!" said the familiar voice. "Let's be on our way."

Donna leapt off the bed and dragged her fingers through her hair. "Oh no," she said, unlatching the door. "I'm not ready! Come in, Gloria. Let me just hop in the shower. I'll be right with you."

"You're not kidding, are you?" groaned Gloria. "Make it quick, and then put on a towel. I'll call Rico and Maddy for triage." Within an hour, Rico and Maddy *had* worked a miracle. Her hair was just right and her clothing elegant but approachable. Just the right combination.

During the intermission of *Whiff and Poof,* Donna stood by the bar at a table decorated with an array of Sinnamon ads, tiny samples, coupons, and other promotions including a huge poster of the ad with Hank kissing Donna.

A handsome man standing in line for refreshments nudged his companion and pointed to the poster. "Have you smelled that yet?" he said.

"Yes," said the friend. "Absolutely incredible. Don't know what it is exactly, but it makes me feel so *righteous* or something."

"I know what you mean," said man number one. "I think I'll

carry some to the UN on Tuesday and see if it helps me with that disarmament thing we're working on."

"Just might do the trick," said his friend.

That little eavesdropping left Donna floating through the evening. All the glad handing was done, in fact, with glad hands. All the broad smiles at strangers were genuine. Her product, her little visiting teaching favor, might help bring about world peace? Oh, it was all worth it! The kids would survive her not being there for parents' night. Instead of sulking, Stephanie would sing for her when she returned. And the dear man in the poster licking chili off her neck would live happily ever after with the lady who helped bring peace to the planet.

This fantasy sustained her through Saturday's commercial shoot and the phalanxes of groupies that now formed everywhere she went. "Oh yes, Sinnamon, yes!" they often said when she signed their match book or their parking ticket or their business card. Each of them thought they were so clever and original. Donna smiled until her cheeks hurt. Sunday at the Plaza was no different. When she entered the dining area, the entire wait staff came out and applauded and introduced a new crepe with a zingy cinnamon glaze, their own nod to Sinnamon's success.

On the plane to Boston, Donna marveled at how true the scripture was that says from small and simple things are great things brought to pass. So many lives enriched by her little invention, so much hope and promise brought by her tiny contribution. Business men feeling "righteous"? Disarmament brought on by the power of a scent? How honorable to be about the Lord's work selling Sinnamon to a needy world.

When she landed in Boston that afternoon, she called home on her cell phone—something Gloria had picked up for her during the week. She got no answer, not even an answering machine. That is so irritating, she thought. What if Gloria was trying to reach me? she grumbled to herself. When she saw Juliet hurrying down the corridor with the kids, she brightened.

94

"Great to see you, Donna!" Juliet said, hugging Donna.

"Mom! Mom!" shouted the boys.

"Celebrity Mother!" sang Stephanie. "You looked so relaxed on *Good Morning America*. How'd you do it? It's had a nice side effect for me, too!"

"What side effect, sweetie?" Donna said. She winced, realizing she'd used a nickname her teenager usually bristled at.

"His name is Kevin Bancroft," sighed Stephanie, nuzzling in closer to Donna.

"Kevin Bancroft?" Donna said, slowing her pace a bit. "Isn't he the quarterback for the football team? The junior? The sixteen-year-old?"

"That's the one, Mom," said Stephanie. "He called yesterday morning and we spent the whole day together down at Quincy Market."

Had Stephanie had two birthdays in her absence? What happened to that policy about not dating until she's sixteen? Donna felt her maternal hackles rising. "And what did your Dad say about this date to Quincy Market?" Donna asked.

"Dad didn't mind. We were going with Roxanne and her boyfriend, Rodney Sullivan, and some of Rodney's friends, but then they decided to go out to Worcester to a gun show. Didn't sound like fun to Kevin or me, so we just spent the day together. He's interested in literature, Mom. Imagine! A football player and smart. He's going to try out for the next school play if it doesn't interfere with his football schedule. And Mom, he's so cute! A little dimple right at the bottom of his chin. Mom, get this! He shaves! Oh, you'll love this! He wants to use Sinnamon for aftershave!" Stephanie sighed, holding Donna's hand tightly.

A headache formed at Donna's brow. Her girl was becoming more affectionate, more communicative about her private feelings than she'd been since she was eight. Was now the time to draw in the reins, to remind her of the no dating until you're sixteen rule?

Quash this tender moment by having Mom-as-Medusa coming so quickly to her lips?

Juliet intervened. "I know a side exit closer to the car. I can see crowds forming up there by the baggage claim. They're all looking your way, Donna. They must be fans. We'll sneak you out here, then we'll be on our way to Wood's Hole. The ferry to Martha's Vineyard leaves at 6:00, so we're in great shape if we don't get waylaid by autograph hounds."

"Cool, Mom!" said Simon, volunteering to haul her wheeled suitcase. "You really *are* famous!"

"Do you think people will send you fan letters?" asked Nate.

"Here comes someone with a microphone, Mom," called Ben.

"Hurry, everybody!" said Juliet. "Out we go!"

"That was fun!" said Ben when they were in Juliet's car and buckled up.

"It's only fun because nobody knows what car we're in or where we're going," said Donna. "It can get pretty tiring."

"I think it's great!" Simon said. "It's like being spies!"

Juliet headed the car south on Rt. 128. No one noticed the blue car following three car lengths behind.

15

"It stinks out here!" Ben said, hugging his arms around himself in the chilly ferry parking lot.

"That's just the sea," said Stephanie.

"That's right, Ben," said Simon. "The smell of rotting fish on a sea breeze is the next smell Mom's going to make."

"He's joking, isn't he, Mom?" said Ben, clinging to Donna.

"You're not going to make us smell dead fish and ask us if it matches something you cooked up, are you?"

"He's kidding, he's kidding," laughed Donna. "Simon, cut it out."

Juliet came out from the ferry office waving the tickets in her hand. "We're all set! Round-trip tickets waiting for us, reserved by Lois!" Juliet said. "Looks like this journey is going to go as smooth as silk."

Right then the blue sedan pulled into the parking lot, crunching the gravel. "Yoohoo! Surprise! It's me!" Margo's voice carried across the parking lot. "Thought you could get away without me, didn't you!"

"Margo!" said Donna, giving her a hug. "This is a surprise! What are you doing down here?"

"Boy, you've got a way with words," said Margo. "What am I doing down here, she asks."

"Hi, Margo," said Juliet, extending her hand.

"Hi, Juliet. I booked a room at Vineyard Haven so, in case you thought I was crashing your party, you have nothing to fear. Just followed you down here from the airport. I thought we could get together for some really quality visiting teaching. Hank told me he couldn't come, so I said to myself, 'Go for it, woman! Get down to the island and party with your friends! So, here I am!"

"I've been looking forward to getting to know you better," Juliet said brightly. "Donna tells me such interesting things about you."

"Interesting? That sounds bad," said Margo.

"No, she brags about your enthusiasm and go-get-'em attitude," Juliet explained. "I see she wasn't exaggerating. I'm glad you came along. It'll be fun."

Disembarking at Vineyard Haven forty-five minutes later, Lois Wheaton met them. "Welcome, welcome! Glad to see things worked out so well. Oh, let's see—another traveler. You look familiar. It's Margo, right?" Lois said.

"I'm impressed," Margo said, "that you'd remember little old me."

"I have a room for you, too," said Lois. "It's nice you came along."

"Thanks," Margo said. "I'll take you up on that."

"We're about a twenty-minute walk from here," Lois explained, "and I have my car for the luggage." Donna opted to walk with the kids. Margo and Juliet rode with Lois in her Jeep. Nate, Simon, and Ben ran back and forth along the shore.

"I wish Kevin could see this—the sea, the spray, the romance of it all," sighed Stephanie.

Just then an attractive teenager on a bike pedaled up alongside Donna and Stephanie on the boardwalk. He hopped off his bike and walked along Stephanie. "Hello, how are you doing this evening?" he said in an Irish accent.

"Hi," said Donna warily. Stephanie waved.

"Aren't you the Sinnamon ladies? You look familiar, ma'am, from the television yesterday, and I spied the poster in the airport. Bought my mom a sample. Are you new to the island? I'm Sean O'Connor visiting from Ireland," he said.

"I'm Stephanie Brooks, from Rottingham," she said.

"My folks are staying up ahead with the Lees. Might you be free this evening?" Stephanie looked at Donna.

"We just arrived, Sean," Donna said. "It's nice to have such a friendly welcome. We're staying with Lois Wheaton, and I'm afraid we're busy tonight."

"Well, she means *she's* busy, but I don't know if I am or not," said Stephanie.

"Steph!" said Donna.

"Isn't that fine. We're right next door to Lois! We'll be cooking outside tonight—barbequing, I think they called it," said Sean. "Roasting pigs or some such outrage!" he laughed. "Come over if you're of a mind. Sure could do with company—someone my age and with such a pretty face. How long are you staying?"

"We go back tomorrow," Stephanie said.

"A shame," said Sean. "Perhaps I'll be lucky and get a second look at you. Good evening to you then." He mounted his bike and rode off.

"Oh, that was nice," said Stephanie. "Wasn't he cute? I loved the accent, didn't you, Mom?"

"He certainly was charming," said Donna. Was now the right moment? "Steph, you remember that we don't date until we're sixteen, right?" Donna asked.

"Oh, Mom, of course I remember," Stephanie said. Without missing a beat, she asked: "So, do you think I can go over to their place tonight?"

"There's Lois up ahead. We'll see what she's got planned," Donna said wearily.

What Lois had planned was a barbeque next door with the Lees. But first they needed to settle into Lois's gracious summer home. Margo began exploring the house, and Donna could tell where she was at any moment because each new discovery was announced with a shriek.

"Look at this, Donna!" Margo howled from the library. "It's a signed photo of Barishnikov sunbathing right here on Lois's front yard! Check out those pecs! ... Oh, I can't believe it! Here's a handwritten recipe from Martha Stewart. Right here in your kitchen, Lois! You know Martha? Really? She's not going to be here this weekend is she? ... Ah, the view! Look at the view!"

"Margo, get a grip," Donna said as they headed to the neighbors' for dinner. "Who knows who might be there tonight. Try and act nonchalant. Don't be all gushy."

"My, have you become one of them now?" Margo said. "I'll try not to embarrass you, but I'm *not* going to act like it's normal to see Barishnikov on your porch. That's your business now, not mine."

"Okay, okay," Donna sighed.

"I'm serious," said Margo. "Off you go to New York and you

don't even call me once. You're living this other life and you don't even share it with me." She said it with a serious, hurt tone.

Donna could hardly speak. "Margo, please ... " she finally managed. But Margo had scurried off ahead to walk with Lois.

"Come in, come in!" said Franny Lee. Franny was a slim, black woman about Donna's age. From her physique, Donna guessed she must be an athlete of some sort. "Lois told us we might get to meet you this weekend," Franny said. "I just love your Sinnamon! I was the first one on the island to have some, and everybody else was jealous."

"We all love it," said Ozzie Lee. There were photos in the living room of Ozzie with a trumpet to his lips and with musicians who were famous enough that even Donna recognized them. "If my horn could make music as sweet and sexy as your Sinnamon, I'd be a happy, happy man!" he laughed. "Can I get you something to drink? Scotch and soda? Gin and tonic?"

"Just a ginger ale would be great," Donna said.

"Yep, that's right," said Margo, suddenly at her elbow. "Donna and I are Mormons. Lips that touch liquor will never touch ours! is what we say." She laughed. Donna laughed, too, but quickly skulked off to watch the kids play with the Lees' dogs and toss the frisbee in the waning light. Was Margo purposely trying to embarrass her?

Juliet came up and handed her a chilled can of ginger ale. "Margo's a lot of fun," she said.

"I guess so," Donna said. "But she comes on a little strong."

"That's just her way, I guess," Juliet said. "We had a nice little visit in the Jeep on the way to the house."

"That must have been, what, about three minutes?" Donna smirked. "That's about the right dose of Margo."

"Juliet, come and see this!" Margo called from the house. Donna watched them. Margo held a big coffee table book of contemporary art on her lap. Juliet sat down next to her and pointed to different pictures. The conversation looked lively, but Donna had no urge to join.

She stood alone on the veranda, sipping her ginger ale. She heard Sean's Irish accent in the fray with the other children's happy, playful noises. She heard the waves lapping not far away at the beach. She watched the sparks from a campfire light up the remaining twilight and scent the air. Her muscles began to relax.

"Have we met?" Donna startled and turned to see a man at her side. He looked vaguely familiar. "Sorry to sneak up on you like that," he laughed. "I know it sounds like a pick-up line, but I feel sure I've seen you somewhere."

"I'm on posters up around town these days," Donna said. That might explain where he had seen *her*, but she still couldn't place where she had seen *him*.

"Not wanted posters, I hope," the man said with a wink. "Or maybe I *do* hope. That would make for an interesting story, wouldn't it?"

"You're the man from the UN!" Donna exclaimed. "I saw you at *Whiff and Poof!* You were standing in line getting a drink when I was at the table with my Sinnamon."

"Oh yes, Sinnamon! Yes! Now I recognize you! *That* poster!" he said. "With the kiss," he added gently. "Quite a captivating photo. Whoever he is, he's a lucky man!"

"That's Hank," said Donna.

"Good for Hank," the man said. "Is he here with you?"

"No," Donna said. "I'm here with my four children. Their dad's back in Boston. We're staying with Lois Wheaton, including a couple of other friends who are here with me—Juliet and Margo—just overnight."

"We have much in common," he said. "I'm here with my children, too. But you've got me beat with the numbers. I have just two—Sean and Eleanor."

"Sean!" Donna said. "Yes, I've met Sean! What a charmer! I thought he said he was from Ireland."

"His mother lives there. I have him and Eleanor for a few weeks."

"He seems to have taken quite a shine to my daughter—my *young* daughter, Stephanie. She's fourteen."

"Sean's sixteen, although he seems to think he's older," the man said.

"One thing Sean knows better than you or I is introductions," Donna laughed. "I'm Donna Brooks."

"Oh, forgive me," said the man. "I was distracted by you and the Sinnamon intrigue! I'm Harris O'Connor. And yes, I do work at the UN. How did you know that, by the way?"

"I eavesdropped," she confessed. "I heard you say something about using it at the UN to work out an arms deal or something."

Harris laughed. "And that I will! We need all the help we can get!"

"It was so flattering to hear. I know it was silly of me and rude to be eavesdropping, but your comment made my day—made my weekend, actually!" she said, looking into his gray eyes—his huge, long-lashed, gray eyes.

"I'd say meeting you is making *my* weekend," he said softly. He looked at Donna and smiled a slow, warm smile, showing perfect white teeth.

He may have been looking right at her, but he didn't see the little figures prancing on each of Donna's shoulders. On one shoulder was an angel dressed in white with a white feathered boa. He whispered, "Listen to the way he's talking. Look how he's looking at you! He thinks you're attractive. Tell him *right now* that you don't accept flattery from strangers."

On the other shoulder was a chubby little devil in a tight red suit. He cooed, "Listen to the way he's talking! Look how he's looking at you! He thinks you're attractive. Enjoy the flattery.

Kick up your heels! It's a party. Nothing wrong with a little conversation."

"Let's take a walk along the shore, shall we?" invited Harris.

"I'd love to," Donna said.

16

A half mile down the shore line, snug in Harris's jacket against the chill of the evening, Donna heard rustling in the beach grass.

"What's that?" she gasped, grabbing Harris's arm.

"Don't know!" said Harris. "Could be anything from mermaids to reporters." Donna suddenly felt self-conscious. She let go of Harris's arm and headed toward the scrubby dune.

"Or a rodent. There's a little flashlight in my jacket—right-side pocket," he said. Donna shone the light in the direction of the sound.

"Stephanie?" Donna said, bewildered, recognizing a face in the vegetation.

"Sean?" said Harris.

"Mom?" "Da?" said the two flustered teenagers.

"What are you doing here?" said Donna.

"Um, we were just exploring the beach, Mom," Stephanie stammered. She wiped her face with the back of her sandy hand.

"Just showing her the vast blue expanse, Da—the sky so starry, the water so alive," said Sean.

"Yeah, yeah, spare me the poetry," Harris said, giving Sean a hand up. "You two will head back to the crowd now. Supper's likely soon. Get along." Sean and Stephanie scrambled off as best they could in the soft sand. They laughed, shaking grit off their jackets and plucking fronds and seaweed off each other.

"Kids!" Harris said, sighing.

"I suppose we should be heading back, too," Donna said,

shaken. "Now what was *that?*" She grabbed onto Harris as a bright light flashed not far away, then a few others in rapid succession.

Harris directed his flashlight at a figure lumbering off down shore with something slung over his shoulder.

"That really *was* a rodent," Harris muttered. "Not to worry. Let's head on back."

" ... and that was when I knew I'd never be a barrel racer in Boise!" said Margo. The crowd erupted with laughter.

"Well, there you two are!" said Ozzie, swinging an arm over Harris's shoulders. "Margo has been captivating us with childhood stories."

"See, Donna?" whispered Margo. "I'm holding my own." Then with her eyebrows raised, she said, "Nice jacket!"

"Oh, Margo," Donna said. "It's all perfectly innocent!"

"Look, Donna. I'm the one who needs a man, and that guy is *gorgeous!* Hand him over!"

"Supper time!" called Franny.

The evening filled with great tastes, ripples of laughter, and frolicsome riffs on Ozzie's jazz trumpet. Sean held forth on the guitar singing gory Irish ballads at Lois's request. Margo recited cowboy poetry she remembered from her childhood. Donna laughed and clapped and soaked in the smells around her of bonfire, salt air, and the sweet, foreign aroma of Harris's pipe tobacco. It was heavenly. Simon, Nate, and Ben played with the Lee kids on the front yard and had to be told three times to come along when it was time to head back to Lois's.

Monday morning Donna woke up late. She could hear the conversation downstairs in the parlor. Juliet, Margo, and Lois were talking about revelation and answers to prayer. Margo shared her lost car keys stories, Juliet confided her conversion experience, and Lois shared a fortuitous premonition at the orangutan reserve. These women seemed engaged and connected. Margo really *was* managing to hold her own.

Should she slip downstairs and chime in? Tell her own spiritual tales? Participate in the little missionary moment happening in the cozy room decorated with photos of muscled ballet dancers and huge glass jars of seashells? Maybe so, but she just couldn't do it. Goblins of worry rose up in her mind, jiggling and prancing for attention. What about Stephanie's turn from literate, somber teen to hormone-driven, flighty kid? Was this because her mother wasn't home enough to lay down the law? Maybe Hank was too lax. Maybe their approach to raising adolescents was from vastly different points of view. What about feeling frumpy and inarticulate and dull when she stayed at home? What about feeling witty, attractive, and valued like Harris made her feel during their little promenade? Did Hank still see Donna as someone valuable? What about people who respected her for her product and sought her approval? *Her* approval, for goodness sake! What about poor innocents like the Borden family who get caught in a media whirlpool against their will? Did she ever follow up on Margo's suggestion to mollify their sorrows with money? No. One more thing slipping through the cracks of her chaotic life. What about Gloria, who arranged her grooming and schedule and her exposure to just the right markets? What about Sister Monson and the biggest, jiggliest gremlin of them all—the Be an Example to the World gremlin? An example of *what* exactly? Donna felt seasick and it was still two hours until the ferry left.

When they arrived back home in Rottingham, Hank opened the door and swung Donna into a tight, passionate kiss.

"Gross, you guys," complained Simon, shoving past them.

"I got sea glass, Dad! Let me show you!" Ben said, trying to yank Hank away.

"I get the remote!" bellowed Nate.

"Did Kevin call?" asked Stephanie.

"You are magic, Donna," Hank said, holding her at arm's length admiringly. "I love you so much, my beautiful, brilliant, wonderful woman. I missed you. Life is dull without you here. *I'm* dull without you here."

Unexpectedly, tears welled up in Donna's eyes. "I love you, Hank," Donna said and drew him into another kiss. "Thank you."

"You're looking a little green," Hank said. "Are you okay? Do you want to lie down a bit?"

"That would be great," she admitted, still woozy from both her funk and the hours of transport.

"I'll warn you that Gloria faxed us a schedule for the next few weeks. I'll let you catch up with that later," Hank said.

"Thanks," Donna said.

"And I want to hear every detail about your Martha's Vineyard trip!" he said, helping her up the stairs.

"Dad, Dad! What's for supper!?" yelled the chorus of young voices.

"They used to nag *me* about that," Donna said wanly.

"You're welcome to the task," Hank said. "I'll hand over the apron tomorrow if you want it back. For now, you get some rest."

"You're a good wife, Hank," Donna chuckled. Hank bowed and headed downstairs. She lay down on the bed without kicking off her shoes. The pillow smelled of Hank, his familiar scent of sweat and soap. Oh yes, Hank, yes.

"Dad, come and look at my shells and glass!" she heard Ben say. "Dad, can Kevin come over for supper?" Stephanie asked. Donna dozed off to the faint sounds of "Dad this" and "Dad that."

When she woke up, it was completely dark except for the glow of the clock face. It read 2:03. She was on top of the covers, though Hank had apparently tossed a quilt over her. Hank slept next to her, sort of, under the sheet and blanket, breathing peacefully, his arm over her waist. She slipped out and groped her way toward the bathroom.

There was a fax from Gloria taped to the mirror, with a little note from Hank: Dear Sleeping Beauty: Boy, were you zonked! I look forward to catching up with you. I look forward to *catching* you! Looks like tomorrow night may be our next chance. Hallelujah you'll be here this weekend! Juliet called tonight. Something about visiting teaching. Tom Borden called. Margo called to say, and I quote, "Tell her I'm sorry again and that I had a wonderful weekend." Sounds like an intriguing story! Sleep as long as you need to. I'll get the kids up and off for school. Love you, your adoring wife—Hank."

Gloria's schedule went all the way to Christmas. The next couple weeks would be mall appearances along the eastern seaboard. Thanksgiving would be at home, but the day after that, the pace picked up again.

Starting November 27th, she had trips to Chicago for an Oprah taping! and to Omaha, Dallas, New Orleans, Seattle, San Francisco, Los Angeles, and last but not least, Salt Lake City. That left a week back in Rottingham for an exhausting array of last minute, on-site interviews and hometown sales just before Christmas.

Hank had circled the Salt Lake City days in red ink: "How about getting together here? Think we can swing it? The kids and I could fly out and join you!"

Donna noticed that after Christmas there was nothing scheduled and she would have her life back. Her good old, settled, predictable life. Thank goodness! It was something to look forward to. No more throngs of groupies or nosey reporters. No more airports. No more lonely hotel rooms. No more bland chit-chat with interchangeable civic leaders. No more schmoozing with famous strangers.

Probably no more big paychecks either, and no more adulation. No more hearty laughter with musicians and tennis champs and diplomats. No more flirtations with handsome strangers. Yes, before she knew it, she'd be back to her settled, predictable life.

17

When Donna woke up, it was sunny. Her stomach felt settled and her funk had lifted. This time the clock read 10:00. Another note in the bathroom indicated that Hank had in fact taken care of the kids and gotten them safely off to school. He left a list of various phone calls to return. She decided to tackle Tom Borden first.

"Hi, Sister Brooks," Tom said. "I just wondered if you knew yet when those posters were going to go away. We keep getting phone calls. It makes Cindy wheezy every time she sees them."

"Look, Tom, " said Donna. "I meant to tell you this earlier, but I've been out of town a lot recently. The poster isn't going to go away ..."

"But Sister Brooks, ..." Tom interrupted.

"Wait a minute, Tom," Donna said. "Let me tell you what I have in mind. It might help." She wished she'd bounced the idea off her lawyer, at least off Hank. Oh, what the heck. She was a big girl now. She could make financial decisions about her own product without consulting somebody else.

"Okay, as I was saying," she continued, trying to sound like she had this all worked out. "I know it doesn't really compensate for using your kids without your permission, but I'm setting up a fund so that 10 percent of my total earnings will go directly to you and Cindy. You can use it for your kids—for their missions, their education, for a few extra trips to Pocatello—whatever you choose. I figure, I give 10 percent to God, and you guys ought to have 10 percent, too."

"Sister Brooks, uh, we never expected ..." stammered Tom. "We just wanted the posters gone. But, I suppose ... why sure, Sister Brooks! That's super! Um, could we have that in writing? I'm sorry to sound so picky, but the last time there was a problem with permissions and all, it just seems ..."

"Sure, Tom, sure," said Donna. "I'll have my lawyer work

something up and deliver it to you." She called Roger Frost's office and made quick arrangements to have it put into action. The next call was to Juliet.

"Sister Young called," Juliet said.

"Sister Young? Sister *Ellen* Young?" Donna asked incredulously. "There was a message on my machine. She called Saturday morning asking for a ride to church on Sunday. We were gone, of course, so I couldn't take her. I thought you said she hadn't been to church in years."

"That's right," said Donna. "I can't believe it! She actually wanted a ride to church? Like to sacrament meeting? Or just to talk to the bishop and complain about something?"

"I don't know," Juliet said. "I wanted to talk to you before I called her. Maybe we can go visit her. Are you free today? I don't have class until 3:30."

"Yeah, today would be great. Give her a call and see what's up," Donna said. A few minutes later, Juliet called back with an appointment, and a half hour later they arrived at Ellen's door.

"Forget I called over the weekend," Ellen said.

"Juliet tells me you wanted a ride to church on Sunday," Donna said. "I'm sorry neither of us was available."

"Oh, don't worry about it," Ellen said, waving her hand vaguely. "Every once in a while I get this craving to hear the hymns of my childhood. But the urge passed. Like gas, you know. While you're here, would you mind making yourselves useful? I want to get some magazines out of my attic for the recycler."

Juliet and Donna exchanged chagrined glances. While they toted string-bound bundles of *National Geographics* out of Ellen's attic, they tried to keep a conversation going.

"*National Geographics*. Do you like to travel?" Juliet asked.

"Not any more," said Ellen. She pointed at the place in the foyer where the bundles should go.

"Did you like to travel when you were younger?" Juliet asked.

"Yes," she said simply.

One thing Donna was learning from her recent experiences with interviews was to ask response questions. Yes or no questions didn't provide much. "What were your favorite hymns as a child?" she ventured.

"Mrs. Brooks," Ellen said sternly. "I asked you two here to help me with this project, not to pry into my life's memories. Let's keep to our task."

The rest of the magazine evacuation effort proceeded in silence. "Thank you, and good day," said Ellen, holding the door open for Juliet and Donna. They were both dripping with sweat despite the autumn chill.

"That's probably the last time she'll let us in," mumbled Donna as she and Juliet approached the car.

"Let's make it mid-month next time," Ellen called from her porch. "None of this end of the month nonsense. I have no use for that." Donna looked at Juliet and rolled her eyes.

They decided to make a quick, unannounced stop at Patty Dominico's. She was there and invited them and fed them more pastries. Afterwards, Juliet asked, "Did you have a good weekend on the island?"

Donna hadn't taken time to think through the weekend's events. "I love the seashore," she said.

"It was fun to get acquainted with Margo. I had thought she didn't like me," said Juliet.

Donna remembered Margo's initial reaction to Juliet but thought it best not to mention it. She diverted the conversation. "I wish I had had more time to talk to Lois. She's quite a woman."

"She really is," agreed Juliet. "We had a great conversation Monday morning while you were sleeping. She has a spiritual core, too, and I had forgotten how much I learn from her. Her spiritual experiences were just like Margo's and mine."

Donna stared at Juliet across the stick shift. "You are amazing, Juliet."

110

"What did I say?" she asked.

"Well, it's just not the standard Mormon line," Donna explained.

"Don't forget, I wasn't raised Mormon, so I probably wouldn't know what the standard line is," Juliet said.

"Oh, come on. You've been in the church long enough to hear it. It's the focus for every lesson on missionary work. We're the ones who have something to teach, not to learn."

"That's just silly," said Juliet. "Of *course* other people have things to teach us. I suppose other people pick up things from us. God is generous, don't you think? Who gets a monopoly on that? Nobody."

"You sound a little, how shall I say this—rare," Donna said.

"You're kidding," Juliet said. "That was something that attracted me to the church in the first place. The missionary quoted Brigham Young, something about 'if there is truth anywhere in heaven, earth, or hell, we claim it.' But Brigham Young was probably 'rare,' too, wasn't he?"

"No argument there," laughed Donna. "As rare as his great-great-great-granddaughter and her *National Geographics* and temperamental orchids."

"While we're talking visiting teaching, I called Tom Borden this morning," Donna said. She rehearsed the situation with the boys' photos and her plan to compensate the family.

"That's generous of you, Donna," Juliet said.

"Well, maybe," Donna said. "I have yet to see a pay check."

That was quickly remedied. The mail lay scattered all over the floor of the entry as usual, and Donna nearly slipped on a glossy Nature Company catalogue. She picked up several envelopes, mostly bills. One of them had Big Apple as its return address and inside was a check for $14,236 for the first month's sales.

There must be some mistake, was the first thing Donna thought, steadying herself against the dining room chair. She

111

called Hank. "You're never going to believe this," she said. She was gasping into the phone. She read him the amount on the check.

"Are you serious?" asked Hank.

"I'm serious!" Donna said. "There's a paper in here with breakdowns from Lucy Hobbes with some of the money taken out for tax and social security and all that. The figure I read you is what we get to keep, Hank. We're going to be rich!"

"That's my gal!" Hank whooped.

"Oh, I did promise the Bordens 10 percent of what I earn as compensation for using their kids."

"You told the Bordens what? Oh, well, 10 percent for tithing, 10 percent for the Bordens, times twelve months in a year ..." Hank quickly calculated. "We're still rich!"

"It's a heap of dough!" Donna squealed.

"A fine heap of cinnamon scented dough!" Hank said.

"Oh yes, Sinnamon, yes!" they both said in chorus.

That evening, to commemorate the occasion, Hank and Donna went out to eat, just the two of them. They ordered in pizza for the kids. With Stephanie grumbling about having to babysit and Simon and Nate grumbling about having to be sat, they slipped away to Legal Seafood again and both ordered lobster—complete with claw crackers, bibs, and tiny forks. For dessert, Hank ate every morsel of Creme Brulee and Donna ordered flourless chocolate cake, practically licking the plate clean. Only five people came up for autographs, and they were staggered enough that they didn't cause a commotion.

"You're smooth, Donna," Hank said, leaning back in his chair. "I've never seen you in action before—this kind of action anyway. You're beautiful and professional," he said. Just then, camera flashes blinded them momentarily. Donna grabbed the wine list to shield her eyes. "Darn those photographers!" she snapped as a few more lights flashed.

A flock of waiters and waitresses trotted briskly down the

aisle toward them. "Oh, no," Donna said. "Not again!" She stood up, threw her napkin down onto her dessert plate, and said: "Can't you folks just leave us alone? I'm trying to have a little private time with my husband!"

Luckily, Hank was the only person who heard her short tantrum. That was because the waiters and waitresses suddenly raised a boisterous operatic version of "Happy Birthday" to a man celebrating with his parents and children at the adjacent table. More cameras flashed. Donna sat down quickly. "You were saying something about how smooth I am?" she groaned.

"You're beautiful when you're red," Hank whispered, taking her hands in his.

"Let's go," Donna said.

"I agree," he said. "Let's go home, uncork a bottle of vintage Sinnamon, and get reacquainted, shall we?"

"Sounds perfect! Have we been gone long enough for the kids to be asleep?"

"It's a school night. Chances are good," said Hank.

But luck was not with them. Stephanie was on the phone giggling. A few weeks ago, Donna would have assumed it was with Roxanne. But these days, who knew? Simon and Nate were in front of the computer yelling, slapping each other's hands off the joystick. Ben was asleep, fully dressed, in front of the TV. On the screen flickered a suggestive video by some heavy metal group.

"What's going on here!" yelled Donna instinctively.

"Off the phone!" Hank told Stephanie unequivocally. He picked up Ben and carried him upstairs.

"You two boys," Donna barked, grabbing the joystick. "Stop your squabbling and clean up this mess! You too, Stephanie! This is terrible! The place is a shambles! You've all got school tomorrow! Look at the kitchen! What were you thinking? What's this garbage on TV? You know better than that!"

Donna was gearing up for another mad rant when Stephanie

stopped her cold. "Great to have you back, Mom," she snarled. "When do you leave again?"

18

Donna's outings the rest of that week were day trips, allowing her to leave after the kids left for school and to get back in time to have a late dinner together. After the ruckus of Tuesday night, everyone was on their best behavior. The house was neater, the phone calls shorter, the homework done promptly. The conversations were polite and efficient.

At first it seemed to be a relief, an emotional ointment. But it was like living in a house of strangers. By the end of the week, Donna actually hummed when she saw the first crumby plate of chips lying on the floor in front of the family-room TV. This was a good sign. A sign of life as she knew it.

On Sunday she was anxious for the comfort of her ever quirky and friendly ward. Had it really only been two weeks since she'd been there? Here at least she knew she would be free from photographers, autograph hounds, reporters. She was ready for a good dose of noisy toddlers, testimonies, and off-key, listless hymn singing—the fond fellowship of the saints.

The kids dashed into the chapel ahead of her. "Ah, the Sabbath," Donna sighed, taking Hank's hand. "A day of rest and renewal. I can really use it."

"I think we all can," said Hank, kissing the top of her head.

In the foyer she saw Adelaide Ottley, a little girl in the Valiant A class, her face pressed against the glass. She had something odd on her head—something gray with a mouthpiece. A walkie-talkie. As soon as Adelaide saw Donna, the girl started jumping up and down.

"Good morning, Adelaide," Donna said "What's that on your head?"

"Sinnamon at the south door! Sinnamon at the south door! Over!" shouted Adelaide into her headset. Soon several Ottley children appeared in the south foyer.

"Sister Brooks! I have to interview you for my high school paper," said Augusta Ottley, a Laurel. "I'm going to follow you around at church today and take notes on you. I get extra credit for seminary for doing this, too. You're so cool, Sister Brooks."

Hank and Donna were soon surrounded by more Ottleys—parents and grandparents—all of them gushing over Donna and her Sinnamon accomplishment. The killer bee cloud of the Ottley family swept Hank and Donna into the chapel and funneled them into the front three rows. Stephanie, Simon, Nate, and Ben gave them quizzical looks from the last row on the right, the usual spot for the Brooks clan. Margo, in the back row of the middle section, gave a perky little wave and smile.

All through the service, Donna felt Augusta's stare and constant note-taking. What could there possibly be to take notes on? Was there a run in her panty hose? Obvious varicose veins? Sister Ottley kept bobbing and smiling at her, bobbing and smiling. The twins drew pictures of Donna in their little Sabbath sketch pads.

After sacrament meeting, Donna and Hank remained encased in Ottleys since the adult Sunday school met in the chapel. Everyone stayed where they were. Augusta stayed, too. Afterwards, the males peeled off with Hank toward the Priesthood room and the female Ottleys escorted Donna to the Relief Society room.

Sister Schmidt conducted. "Glad to have you all here. A few announcements. Start thinking ahead for our Sub for Santa collections for the Lake Avenue Shelter. Be sure to contact Gladys Brockbank to make your donations beginning Thanksgiving weekend. Karma and Hjalmar Caputo just had their first baby, a little girl they've named Pluto. Weighed in at 9 lbs. 2 oz. I'm sure the Caputo family would appreciate some help with meals for a few days, so Sister Christiansen is passing around a list. And sisters, when you drop off your food, please be discreet and don't laugh at the baby's name.

"Enrichment is next week on Thursday the 12th. Sign-ups are going around. There are three classes. One will be on Christmas crafts, and you'll need to bring lace, ribbons, and tampons for that one. The second class is about how to make good use of things that expire in the back of your fridge. The last class is a slide show on fashion called "From Twiggy to Fabio.""

Donna might have enjoyed the Relief Society lesson on new approaches to reverence by one of the brighter bulbs in the ward, but she felt the eye of Augusta on her. As soon as the closing prayer was "amened," Donna stood up and told the young reporter that she really *had* to get to the bathroom immediately. Augusta, of course, jotted that down since it was the first real quote she had gotten.

Donna elbowed her way quickly and politely through clusters of folks who were attending to church business and people who wanted to detain her to chat about Sinnamon. She shoved open the door to a ladies room in a deserted corner of the church and took refuge in the farthest stall. She hadn't really needed to use the facilities, but she needed the escape. The tiny cubicle was the definition of claustrophobic to most people, but it was like a pocket of fresh air to her.

She sat there with her hands tented over her nose breathing deeply in and out. She shut her eyes and tried to recreate the gentle lapping of the waves on Martha's Vineyard. Yes, that was a good, calming rhythm. In and out, in and out, steady and serene.

After several silent minutes, she was becoming mellow, ready to meet the throngs again, when the door suddenly burst open with the arrival of a chatty group of young women, three of them, Donna guessed. They didn't use the stalls but stood, probably primping and combing their hair in the mirror. Donna didn't want to look out between the gaps.

"Did you see Sister B. on that poster downtown?" said one girl. Donna's ears perked up.

"Sure! Who would think a lady that old and so plain looking would be in a gushy shot like that! To tell you the truth, the picture gives me the creeps."

"And you remember all those kids in the picture? Whose babies were those? I recognized Stephanie—how embarrassing for her, can you imagine?—but who were those other, little kids?"

"Oh, didn't you hear? They borrowed the Borden twins for the photo but didn't tell the Bordens what they were doing. Now Sister B. has to pay them with some big scholarship fund or something."

"That's pretty cool."

"I'll tell my Dad about that because he's looking for funds. If she's got money to throw around like that, he ought to hit her up."

Donna kept as still as she could. The conversation turned to school work and TV shows, and soon the trio left. Donna heaved a long sigh and practiced some more deep breathing. Another group came in. This time it was older women, and they were noisier and used every faucet and feature in the room.

"What a spectacle! She's sure got the Ottleys under her influence, doesn't she?" (Door clanking and a bolt slipping into place.)

"Did you notice how they abandoned their children today—left them sitting alone in the back? No good can come from that kind of thing." (Whirr and rattle of the paper dispenser. Flush. Door opening.)

"Absolutely. Do you remember her giving a talk in church last month? There was a photographer there. I think it was some kind of publicity stunt." (Water running.)

"How do you figure?"

117

"I mean, it was supposed to be a youth talk—like she quali-fies! I think she wanted to show off for the photographer, and she probably wanted to remind us to buy her Sinnamon product, too." (Water off. Towel yanking.)

"That sounds far-fetched to me, Verna. I mean, the photog-rapher didn't take any pictures." (Whirr, flush, bang.)

"Yeah, but think about it. Do you remember what she said in her talk?" (Water running. Soap dispenser surging. Water run-ning again.)

"That was weeks ago." (Water running. Paper towel yank-ing.)

"I can remember it because I had a feeling she might be up to something. It was about the wise men and their gifts. Wise men? Gifts? In September? It was a marketing ploy!" (Purse snapping. Hair brush in motion.)

"Gifts?"

"Sure, gift giving! Sinnamon! And right after that, she shows up on every street corner with that lurid poster! I think she should have her recommend taken away for ... exploiting the church or something." (Whirr, flush, bang.)

"Oh, Verna, you're a hoot!" (Water running. Towel yanking. Door to the ladies room closing.)

Donna's shoulders sank. She stopped trying to breath deeply. She stopped trying to do anything and simply waited until it was quiet for several minutes. Then she went out and found the car full of grumpy kids and a grouchy Hank. "Where have you been?" they griped in chorus.

That afternoon she called Margo. "Come over, Margo. I need a distraction, and you're good for that," Donna said.

"Thanks, I guess. I'll be right over."

Donna told Margo about the conversations in the bathroom.

"I guess this kind of life has its down side, doesn't it? It's not all rosy having to put up with that kind of rudeness. Not that I don't feel jealous myself, mind you."

118

"I guess it's got its perks," Donna said. "But right this very minute, I'd rather be anonymous."

"That's not likely from what I know of your schedule," Margo said.

Donna showed Margo the plans for December.

"Gee, girlfriend. I don't know when I'm even going to see you. Look at this craziness!"

"There are a few days here and there," Donna said. "Besides, I still have you on my visiting teaching route."

"That's true," Margo said. "Hey, you were right about Juliet. She can be a little dry, but she's alright, isn't she? We're so different. She's blue-blood, and I come from a cowboy family. But she doesn't seem to care."

"I told you that you might like her," Donna said.

"I can't figure out why exactly," Margo mused. "I guess it's because she appreciates my goofiness. Do you think your ad people might have a need for that kind of thing? How about a sketch with an academic and a cowgirl, and they both like Sinnamon?"

"You don't give up, do you, Margo?" Donna said. They laughed. In fact, they laughed so loud, the kids came running into the room to see what was up.

Margo stayed for dinner—a chicken and pesto pizza that Donna prepared this time. "They put these caramelized onions on the pizza at room service at the Plaza," Donna said. "I think I copied them pretty well here."

"Kevin would like this," said Stephanie. "I ought to do like you and Dad and put some pizza sauce behind his ear."

"Kevin?" Margo said. "Who's Kevin? What happened to Sean?"

"Who's Sean?" asked Hank.

"He's a guy we met on Martha's Vineyard who had the hots for Stephanie," Simon said.

"Really?" Hank said, raising his eyebrows and smiling. "You

know, it's been a week now and I still haven't heard any details about this trip of yours."

"Margo, you're the master at bullet points," said Donna. "How would you sum it up?"

"Obnoxious stalker follows rising celebrity to a get-away weekend and makes a nuisance of herself," Margo began. "Repents and patches things up."

"Right," Donna said. She tossed a heel of bread at Margo. "Don't forget 'rising celebrity acts like a know-it-all and neglects her best friend. Also repents.'"

"High profile femmes share spiritual secrets," Margo continued.

"That sounds interesting," Hank said.

"Sounds like a *National Inquirer* title, but it was really more like something from the *Church News*," Margo explained.

"More, Margo!" urged Nate. "More!"

"Okay. Boys cavort with frisbees and retrievers."

"Yeah!" said Nate and Simon.

"Young beachcomber makes colorful discoveries," said Margo, ruffling Ben's hair.

"That's me, Dad. The sea glass. Remember? That stuff is neat!"

"Girls cavort with Irishmen."

"Girls? There was more than one Irishman?" Hank interrupted.

"Yeah, Sean's father is a UN diplomat and quite a looker. He and Donna had a nice little moonlit stroll down the strand."

"It was nothing, Hank," said Donna.

"Then why are you blushing?" Hank asked.

"But our Donna was the paragon of virtue and wholesomeness," Margo quickly added.

"This paragon of virtue and wholesomeness is getting bored by this storyline," Donna said as she snuggled closer to Hank. She struck her finger along her greasy pizza plate and wiped it behind

Hank's ear. As he started to complain, she gave him a juicy kiss. "Oh yes, caramelized onion, yes!"

The first three weeks of November required careful balance. On Thursdays Donna gave the kids a snack when they came home from school and then left. She returned Sundays around dinner time. Before long, every town from Maine to Miami was a blur to her. Another check arrived, and they decided to hire somebody to come and clean the house. That proved to be more trouble than good since in her thoroughness, the cleaning woman threw out Stephanie's scattered notes for her history paper. They decided to return to the original plan of saving money and trying to tolerate the squalor.

Over the next few weeks, Donna noticed that it wasn't just the house that seemed a little off. The kids argued more and were slower to respond. They opted for TV instead of books or creative projects or outdoor activities. They clearly drifted toward Hank when they needed help finding something, including an after-noon snack or some light conversation or an extra hug. For his part, Hank managed to stay upbeat and supportive about Donna's schedule, with very few exceptions.

"How do you do it, Hank?" Donna asked him that Sunday after supper.

"I remind myself that before long, this will all be over. It's not bad for a short haul," he said, drawing her close to him. "I've learned a lot about what you have to put up with at home and how hard your job is. It's kind of like a fast. But I have the luxury of knowing it won't last forever," Hank said. "It helps me to be generous knowing that you'll be the prime fetch-and-carry girl in just a few weeks."

Donna poked him in the ribs. "We'll see about that. There's some serious room for negotiation on the chore front, don't you think?

"Yeah, I suppose you're right," Hank said.

"How did I get so lucky?" Donna asked.

"Don't know," Hank said.

The doorbell rang. Donna went to answer it.

"Donna! Oh, I'm so glad I found you. I've missed you! Pardon my being so bold, but I've been thinking about you since we had those few hours together. I wasn't sure how to locate you. Sean told me Stephanie said she lived in Rottingham, and since I'm here working with the Irish Consulate in Boston this weekend, I just wanted to take the chance ... Oh, here I am babbling when what I really want to do is this ..."

With that, Harris O'Connor dropped a bouquet of roses at Donna's feet, then he took her face in his hands and planted an impassioned kiss right on her mouth.

19

"Allow me to introduce myself," Hank said firmly, stepping around Donna. "I'm Donna's husband, Hank. And who might you be?"

Harris jumped back. "Oh my, I'm so sorry."

"Oh, Harris," Donna said. He was as red as the little devil had been that night on her shoulder. "It's so wonderful to see you again. This is awkward. Yes, well. You remember Hank from the poster?"

Harris looked pale, his expression blank. "Oh yes," he said. "From the poster. The Sinnamon poster." He took Donna's hands, then self-consciously dropped them. "I'm so sorry; I misunderstood." Then to Hank, "I'm sorry, Mr., um, Brooks. I've been terribly improper here."

Through all of the stumbling and fumbling, Hank's color was cooling from his initial deep rage purple to more natural tones. "Well, Donna did mention something about a charming little Irishman. I suppose you're the guy," Hank said.

"Charming? ... Yes, well, that's very kind. But as you can see, charmers have our tactless side, too. Let me assure you, Mr. Brooks, that nothing untoward was intended."

"Why don't you step in," said Hank, to Donna's surprise.

"That's awfully gracious of you," Harris said. He stooped down and picked up the flowers. "These are—were—for you. Perhaps we should change that now. Should we say they were from Sean to Stephanie? He wanted me to bring her a little something. Would that please her?"

"She'd be thrilled. I'll go put them in some water," Donna took a quick escape. In the kitchen, she picked up the phone and hit Margo's instant dial button.

"Harris O'Connor is here," she whispered.

"Who?" Margo said.

"Harris! The UN guy! Hank's with him in the living room! Get over here quick!" Donna said. She hung up the phone and went back carrying the vase of flowers into a silent living room. "Stephanie! Boys! Come to the living room," Donna called. "Mr. O'Connor is here." The boys arrived, said hello, and left again. Stephanie galloped down the stairs from her bedroom.

"Hi, Mr. O'Connor! How's Sean?" Stephanie asked.

"These flowers are from him," Harris said.

"You must have made quite an impression, Steph," said Hank.

"Flowers? Oh, wait till Kevin hears about this. He'll be sick!" She waltzed back up to her room holding the vase carefully in front of her.

"Again, Mr. Brooks," Harris began. "This really is quite embarrassing. In my line of work, we pride ourselves on creating peace rather than havoc."

The doorbell rang. "Hi guys!" Margo said, swooping into the room. "I just made this nummy dessert and thought I'd bring it over. Oops! You have company?"

123

"Come in, Margo! Come in," said Donna and Hank in unison.

"What is it? Spoons or forks?" Hank asked.

"Pumpkin cheesecake," Margo said. "Forks will do. You're Harris, aren't you? We met last month at Martha's Vineyard."

"Oh yes, Margo. I remember you well. Let's see, 'When up in the saddle I stare at the sky ...'" he quoted.

"I can't believe you remember that," Margo laughed, settling in next to him on the couch. "Can you believe that he remembered that silly cowboy poem? You may be a diplomat, but your life is way too small if you're memorizing cowboy poems."

"But you memorize cowboy poems," said Harris.

"Honey, my life is so small," Margo began, "it would make a gnat feel claustrophobic."

Everyone laughed and Donna said a silent prayer of gratitude for her good friend Margo. She said another prayer that Harris might cast those gorgeous gray eyes Margo's way.

The pumpkin cheesecake was delicious. The boys ventured up again and were cute. Stephanie ventured down and actually sat next to Donna and added pleasant comments to the conversation. Margo was funny and flirty. Harris, in fact, seemed charmed by her.

That night Donna tried to explain a little more about the Vineyard interlude, but Hank put a finger, then a kiss, to her lips.

"I'm a saint," Hank said. "I know. I know. Besides, I could have beaten him up if I had wanted to."

The next few weeks were dizzy with airports, appearances, interviews, and limos. Sister Monson left messages amounting to scoldings at every hotel where she stayed: "You should have slipped in some mention of the church welfare program ... You missed an opportunity to talk about food storage and how it applies to your product, Sister Brooks. Another opportunity lost! ... When are you going to emphasize the church, Sister Brooks? I

124

think you're being remiss ... Such an easy opening to talk about the temple, and you let it slide right through your fingers!"

Donna didn't want to follow Sister Monson's suggestions, but it did turn her to prayer. She tried to listen to what the Spirit told her to say at every interview. So far, it had never once urged her to break out into singing "Come, Come Ye Saints." Besides, there was a trip to Salt Lake City coming up and that would certainly be the prime time to mention her religion. Did people really care what denomination any celebrity was? It seemed to her that John Travolta didn't fare too well when his religious beliefs came up in the news, did he? She recalled that Sammy Davis Jr., God rest his soul, had some affiliation, but she could no longer remember what it was. Relying on the Spirit would just have to do.

There were a few highlights that made the various cities distinct from one another. In Chicago at the gift shop at the top of the Sears Tower, a young woman with a nose ring, eyebrow ring, and probably rings in less obvious spots purchased fifteen bottles of Sinnamon. "They're for my coven," she said shyly when Donna asked her about her bulk buy.

A restaurant in New Orleans welcomed her by spelling out "Sinnamon" in crawdads at the luncheon buffet. A Lebanese cab driver in San Francisco didn't recognize her but smelled so strongly of Sinnamon that she thought he must have marinated himself in it. He had a little vial hanging up with his fuzzy dice. She was weak when she got out of the car. "These steep hills will get you every time when you're new to the city," the driver said, helping her out. She left him a substantial tip and then walked around the block to clear her senses.

Thursday morning, December 17th, she headed to Salt Lake City for her next assignment. Her reservations were for the Inn at Temple Square for Thursday and Friday nights, and Hank and the kids would join her Saturday to head up to Snowbird, the ski lodge.

"You're on a roll here, Donna," said Gloria on one of her touch-base phone calls. "The final stretch! Oh, while you're in Salt Lake, go ahead and mention your church connection. It'll probably boost sales there to know that they're supporting one of their own."

Gloria didn't need to make the suggestion. The reporters in Salt Lake had done their homework, or Sister Monson had done it for them. "Sister Brooks," asked one shiny faced reporter at a BYU Business School seminar Thursday afternoon. "How have you managed to juggle home life with your rapid rise to fame?"

Donna wished she had a volume button on the voice of the Spirit because reception wasn't very good. "I, um, have a very supportive family. My husband has taken up a lot of the slack and my kids are resilient."

"Sister Brooks, what have been your primary investment strategies with your new-found income?" asked an eager young woman who actually had a pencil behind her ear.

Donna's impulse was to say, "None of your business, dear," but she figured that wasn't polite. "We have our children's long term interests in mind, of course. My husband and I make these decisions together." Was that bland enough to say nothing much but satisfy their snoopiness?

"What do you think about yourself as a role model for women?" asked another.

"I have a hard time thinking of myself as a role model at all. I'm just Donna Brooks, a homemaker from Rottingham, Mass."

The Q&A session reviewed nicely in the next day's paper. "Humble homemaker shares fame and glory with family ... Assertive, yet kind, this ambitious woman keeps it all together—career, kids, and candor ... Hey, Salt Lake! This devoted Mormon homemaker and mother of four is *our* Ms. Brooks!"

Friday morning Donna faced cameras again for an interview with Channel 5. The anchor looked about twenty-five, was well scrubbed, well built, and had a head covered with cherubic blond curls. "Tell us about your favorite callings in the church, Sister Brooks … How do you enjoy living in the mission field? … How do you feel about standing up for home and family outside of Zion where there's so much moral decay? … Share with us some missionary experiences that have come your way because of your involvement with Sinnamon."

Missionary experiences? The nose-ringed bulk-buy for the coven wouldn't count, would it? And would it take too much explaining to go into stories about lost keys and orangutan preserves? She chose to answer with something she remembered Juliet said. "Other people have so much to teach us, lessons about life and relationships and creativity. God is very generous. No one has a monopoly on truth. That was something Brigham Young taught, and I'm with Brother Brigham on that score."

The questions went on and on. Some could be fielded cheerfully and forthrightly. Others were so arrogant or insipid that she had to try instead to answer the questions the reporter should have asked.

Question: "Sister Brooks, if you, yourself, were a smell, what would you be?"

Response: "Yes, Sinnamon may in fact be a simple little item—a handy stocking stuffer for everyone on your list, but I believe that from small and simple things can come great things. My intention was to provide a gentle but emphatic little reminder of deeply good things of comfort, connection, and warmth. When people feel confident of those things, we all get along better; we are kinder to each other. No, it's not a cure for cancer, but it really can make this a happier, friendlier world to live in."

Question: "What was your first thought when you knew Sinnamon was going to make you rich and famous?"

Response: "No, I don't have any plans to market more scents beyond Sinnamon. I hadn't even initially intended to market this one, but when the opportunity presented itself, I realized that a simple item that could make people happy was worth sharing. I have no other products on the drawing board at this time."

This was a taped interview. She knew from the *Entertainment Tonight* experience what wonders a creative video editor could do. They could patch things around with abandon.

After all of this, she couldn't wait to put her feet up, turn on the cable in the hotel room, and wait for Hank and the kids to arrive the next day. She chose the History Channel so she wouldn't have to see herself on the news that night. But Saturday morning when she opened the paper, there was a half-page photo of her with the curly-haired anchor: "Sinnamon Lady Lives Brother Brigham's Message: Tolerance, Curiosity, Commitment." That sounds great, Donna thought to herself. Did I really say that?

Someone knocked at the door. There was the bellboy holding a huge floral arrangement. "Thank you!" she said, slipping him a tip. She read the card. "Thanks for your good work and for adding celestial spice to all our lives—the Public Affairs Department."

That was nice of Sister Monson, Donna thought. And very friendly, given the tenor of her recent messages. Then she realized it wasn't from Sister Monson. It was from THE Public Affairs Department. The one for the whole church a block east on North Temple Street!

The phone rang. "Donna Babe! Gloria here at Big Apple. Lucy just handed me the morning stats. You've knocked their stuffy little socks off! Sales this morning for the Intermountain region are fifty times higher than they were last week! What a woman! Keep at it! Tuesday morning you can go back home, take a deep breath, and get ready to rock and roll for those last two days before Christmas!"

Donna checked out and took the shuttle to the airport disguised in dark glasses, a baseball cap, and a jacket with the collar pulled up around her cheeks. It worked well. No one recognized her. Hank and the kids came through the gate at the airport and

Donna ran to them. She whispered into Hank's ear, "I'm the toast of the town! Look at this!" She stuffed the newspaper into his hands and went to hug the kids.

"Hi, you guys! You look terrific," she said. "Ready to have some holiday fun?" she asked as they climbed into the Ford Explorer that Gloria had arranged for them.

"It's already fun! We're out of school until January!" said Nate.

"Where are we going to stay, Mom?" Ben asked.

"We're going to stay in a ski lodge for a few days," Donna said.

"Do they actually have snow up there?" Hank asked. "It's so dry down here."

"Supposed to be a good fifteen feet or so. That's what they tell me anyway."

"Great, Mom!" said Stephanie. "I can't wait! I've never really been skiing before!"

"What do you mean? You've been skiing in New Hampshire," Donna corrected.

"Well, Mother, that's not *real* skiing," she said.

The car ride was relaxing and pleasant. The kids regaled her with tales of their most recent school pranks and parties. Stephanie stared out the windows and sighed at the spectacular scenery. There was definitely snow. Donna was glad Hank was at the wheel so she could pay full attention to the kids.

Hank pulled the Explorer into the parking lot at the lodge and started collecting luggage and heading off to the check-in counter. Donna struggled with her wheeled cart. One of the wheels was wedged in under the seat-belt cartridge. She yanked. It budged a little. She yanked again, and this time the suitcase flew out the back of the car. She tried to grab onto something stable to catch her fall, but nothing presented itself. Down she went on the icy patch behind the Explorer. Down she went in an ambulance with EMTs to get her broken foot set at the nearest hospital.

20

The emergency room seemed to take forever. So much for the sunglasses and baseball cap disguise. When the hospital personnel had her identity, it became a publicity free-for-all. Photographers hovered outside the ambulance and jostled each other outside the x-ray room. They flocked around the Explorer as Hank drove in.

Four excruciating hours later, Donna and Hank returned to Snowbird Lodge. It was past midnight and, thankfully, there was no obvious press corps on hand. Donna appreciated the painkillers and the groggy little high they left her with.

When she awoke Sunday morning at nearly 11:00, the kids were off at the bunny slopes and Hank lay by Donna's side flicking channels with the remote.

"Hey, my adorable little snow bunny," he teased. "Good morning to you!"

"My foot feels like it's the size of a watermelon."

"It probably is from the look of those five purple sausages sticking out of the cast," he said. "How you feeling?"

"Like a total klutz. A klutz in pain. How about another one of those pain killers?"

Hank shook two into her hand and got her a glass of water. "Okay, lady. You lie there and I'll read the paper to you."

"Sounds good," said Donna, leaning back on the pillows.

"The *Salt Lake Tribune* leads with 'Sinnamon Lady Rises in Sales but Slips at Slopes!'"

"Oh, no," Donna groaned. "They thought this was newsworthy?"

"They've got a picture of you in the ambulance waving and smiling through the window." He held the paper for her to see.

"I waved and smiled?"

"Yes, indeed," Hank said. "And this is pretty newsy actually, more about the economics of the product than your fall. Besides, the headline makes it sound like you were skiing."

"Does it say that I just fell on my tookus pulling a suitcase out of the car?" Donna asked.

Hank scanned the article. "No mention of any tookus. Next is the *Deseret News* with an alliterative banner: 'Brooks Breaks Bone, Bears Up Buoyantly.'"

"Bears up buoyantly? I feel like I've been run over!" she groaned.

"That may well be, but apparently in your hour of desperation, you were kind to everybody. There's another perky shot of you here. See?"

"They must have had me on morphine early," Donna said. "I'd better call Gloria. This is going to affect the rest of the schedule."

"She called this morning while you were sleeping and said to just keep your feet up. They'll make sure you get a good wheel chair when you need it. The camera shots will all be waist up."

"Makes me wonder what they were focusing on before," Donna said. "Sounds like she's not giving me any recovery time, though, is she? She really said to keep my feet up? How clever of her."

"Oh, here's a little news flash I passed on to Gloria when she phoned," Hank added. "There was a call this morning from the owner of Snowbird, and he says they'll cover all our expenses— the kids' skiing lessons, the spa, the arcades, our meals, even pop from the soda machines."

"That's generous!" Donna said.

"Yes, but he also said that since the papers came out this morning, they've been getting constant calls for reservations. He

131

thinks they'll be booked up for the next three months. He also placed an order to hand out Sinnamon with the soap and shampoo. If you had to fall and break your foot, Donna, you picked a great place to do it! You've made the place famous!"

"I'll bet he's just doing this so we don't sue him for the ice in the parking lot," Donna said.

"Haven't you become cynical," said Hank.

"I guess I've spent too much time in New York. It's wearing off. Or because of that screw-up with the Borden kids and wondering if they would sue us," Donna said.

"I saw the Bordens at church last Sunday. They both came up and shook my hand and thanked me, thanked me, thanked me. I could hardly get them to let go. They said they're on their way to Pocatello for the holidays. Cindy and the kids are going to stay out there until the baby comes and he's going to fly out on the weekends. They're very happy, Donna, and everybody's breathing easily. Literally."

"That's good to hear. Hank, I'm getting sleepy again. Do you think we should try to gather the kids and go down to church somewhere?"

"Church? With you in this condition? I think we can play hooky today. Let's just plan on being at the Christmas Carol Sing-In at the ward, like we always do, and count that as church. Is that a good plan?"

"Okay, I guess so," said Donna yawning. "Why don't you go off skiing? Take advantage of the mountains. Keep the remote near me in case I wake up, but I'm not good for much."

"I think I will hit the slopes for a while," Hank said.

"Make sure you put sun block on your nose and backs of your ears. What about the kids? Did they put on sun block? Do they have keys to get in? When will they be back? Is there enough to entertain them?"

"What a mother you are!" Hank laughed. "Everything's fine.

We'll all meet back here at 6:00 and wheel you out for dinner. How's that sound?"

"Great! Now go out there and have some fun!" she said.

"Yes, ma'am!" said Hank. He kissed her on the forehead and headed out the door.

The rest of the day passed in a fog. Donna recalled something about Stephanie spending time in the parlor with a seventeen-year-old from Orlando who recognized her from the poster. Fine, Donna thought. The parlor is public. That's okay. She heard her boys were playing arcade games almost non-stop, courtesy of Snowbird Lodge, and that they thought their garlic mashed potatoes at dinner were gross. Hank bragged about some tricky slopes he had conquered. Donna was happy that he was getting out and enjoying himself and not spending time nursing her. Her swelling was going down and the pain was abating. But she still needed a pill, especially toward the end of the day when she was most worn out. She made one brief hobble with her crutches out onto the balcony to enjoy the view, but she soon felt woozy again and retreated back to the couch.

That's about all she could recall. She enjoyed the stupor of staying indoors and watching *I Love Lucy* reruns and national weather surveys. The torpor was such a pleasant switch from the manic mode Gloria typically had her on.

The next morning after Hank and the kids left for the slopes, Donna called down to the front desk for a couple of extra newspapers. She was itching for some crossword puzzles and "Dear Abby." A few minutes later there was a knock at the door, although by the time Donna made her way to open it, there was no one there. But a stack of newspapers lay at the threshold, including three tabloids. The trick was getting down to pick them up. She managed this acrobatic stunt by sitting on the floor, pulling the papers into her lap, and awkwardly shutting the door again. She didn't want to hoist herself up, so she leaned over to pick up a pencil on the floor by the couch and then nestled back against the low pine dresser. She settled in for her anticipated pleasures.

As she unfolded the papers and read the big, bold headlines on the tabloids, her heart stopped. "Exposé: Model Mormon Mom Has Seaside Tryst! *Sin*ammon Earns Its Name!" The accompanying photo was of Harris O'Connor, cheek to cheek with Donna on Martha's Vineyard Island.

"Wholesome Is a Hoax: Sinnamon Teetotaler Tipsy!" This story had a picture of a mad-eyed Donna peering over the top of a wine list at Legal Seafood. Next was "Pill Popping Perfume Peddler is High in the Mountains!" This one showed a bedraggled Donna staring with glazed eyes from the Snowbird Lodge balcony.

It took her some time to take in what she saw. Before she knew what had happened, hot tears began rushing down her cheeks. She felt as if the glue holding her joints together had dissolved. She sagged toward the dresser, propped only by the geometry of her bones. She stared straight ahead through a foggy film of tears and noticed absently that there was a knot in the shape of a letter *J* directly opposite her in the paneling.

She had no idea how long she sat like this, vacant and moist and limp. Maybe an hour. Maybe more. Eventually, when her foot started throbbing, she became aware of pain. It was welcome, an indication of all her hurts. Soon she could identify points of injury. How would her children feel when they saw these awful photographs and read these vicious words? How abandoned, how betrayed would they feel? And Hank? Would he still trust her? Would he want to run away as fast as he could? What about her friends, everyone who knew and trusted her? How would they ever be able to look her in the eye again and not wonder who she really was? What about those poor sweet folks like the Ottleys and all the other gushy ones who idolized her? Would it crush their hearts? Or worse yet, would they not be able to differentiate her scandal from the church? Would she and her family have to move out of Rottingham and assume new identities? Or would her family stay, constantly beating down the brand of shame? Would she be cast out all alone? And all of this—this grief, this crisis—because of these foolish, lying photos and stories.

But wasn't *she* the real fool because she bought into this in the first place? This frolic with fame, this dalliance with the devil? She hadn't meant for this to happen. None of these things *did* happen, not in the way they were being spun out. But would her knowing that convince anyone? Was the breach too great? Was there too much harm done—too much betrayal? Hank, the children—how will they cope with this embarrassment?

For another hour, Donna lay there crying and festering in heartache. Her nose was running but she had no will or energy to do anything about it. It must have been around 11:00 when Hank opened the door and found Donna in that state.

"Donna! What happened?" he cried, sweeping her up off the floor. He positioned her on the couch, propping big cushions behind her head. "What happened? Is it your foot? Did you take too many pills? Should I call the doctor?"

"Mom, Mom? Are you okay?" The kids flocked around her smoothing her hair, offering her tissues.

All Donna could do was point vaguely at the papers on the floor. "Take a look at those," she said weakly.

"What in the world is this?" Hank bellowed.

"What is it, Dad?" "Lemme see, lemme see!" the kids clamored.

Hank sat down by Donna and turned the pages and the kids stared over his shoulder, gasping. "What's that picture of you, Mom? Who are you with?" asked Simon. "He looks sort of familiar."

"That ... that must have been that rodent on Martha's Vineyard," Donna said in a barely audible voice.

"I wasn't thrilled that he kissed you, Donna," Hank said, "But I wouldn't call Harris a rodent."

"Who kissed Mom?"

"That guy in the picture?"

"That's Sean's Dad!"

"Did you have an affair, Mom?"

"No! We were out by the shore and it was cold. He gave me his coat. Then I saw a light go off. I didn't see what it was, and Harris just said it must have been a rodent. I think he meant one of those paparazzi guys!"

"Look at this one!" said Hank, starting to laugh. "This was when you got mad in Legal Seafood."

"What did she do, Dad?"

"She grabbed something to hide behind—the wine list! See?" Hank said, pointing to the paper. "Right there! This is so funny!"

"And that one, Mom," said Stephanie, starting to chuckle, too. "That's you on the balcony last night! Ha, ha, ha!"

"Look how they're blowing this into some kind of scandal!" Hank laughed.

"How can you laugh?" Donna cried. "This is *me* they're lying about! This is *us*! People are going to believe this stuff! And they've taken something simple and fun like Sinnamon and our little marketing campaign and made it seem all tawdry and sleazy like some cheap trick! They make *me* seem like some cheap trick! Whatever good I did for the church is totally down the drain now!"

The phone rang. Hank picked it up. He put his hand over the mouthpiece. "It's Gloria. Can you talk to her?"

Donna wiped her eyes and tried to control the quaver in her voice. "Hullo," she sniffed.

"Don't worry, Donna," Gloria said soothingly. "We've seen them. Yes, they're awful but ..."

"I really didn't ... I never ... I'm not ... !" Donna broke into another wave of angry tears.

"Listen, it's okay," Gloria said. "Now, this is what we've got in mind. I know you're not very mobile, but we want to send an

136

interview team up to meet you there at Snowbird. They'll arrive in about an hour. So what you need to do is spruce up, splash some water on your face, and let 'em have it with both barrels! This is your chance to set the record straight! Don't worry, Donna."

"But Christmas is right around the corner, and with this awful mess, no one will want to buy ..." Donna sniffled.

"This is playin' with the big boys, Donna," Gloria said. "Remember how you wouldn't let Rico push you around? These lousy photographers and cheap tabloids are just like Rico—even worse. But you can handle them! Shake it off, Donna. It's okay."

Donna hung up the phone and wiped the tears off her face. She didn't know Gloria could be so warmhearted. It takes a stressful situation to bring out the best in people, she thought. Hank held her in his arms and rocked her. The kids examined the papers, snickering and pointing.

Donna hobbled to the bathroom to tidy up. She took one look at her swollen face and knew she needed help. "Steph," she called. "Can you give me a hand here?"

Twenty minutes later Donna emerged with her hair washed and blown dry and styled smartly. Her make-up was maybe just a little more blushy than Donna would have chosen, but given the puffy eyes, it was probably for the best.

"You look great, Mom," Stephanie said, actually kissing her on her reddened nose.

"I owe it all to you!" Donna returned. She settled herself in the large rocker by the TV and propped her foot up on the hassock.

The phone rang. Hank answered it. "It's the front desk. The interview crew is here. They're on their way up."

Donna looked around at her family and felt herself coming to life. No one—no bossy wardrobe man, no rigid church lady, no money grubbing paparazzi—*no one* is going to invade my life, Donna thought. Nobody has a right to twist and turn it like some theme-park balloon. Let me at 'em. I'm loaded for bear!

21

When Gloria said "interview crew," it was an inadequate term. This was an infestation of buzzing, clicking, trampling hordes who tangled equipment and moved like grasshoppers on pioneer crops. Wave after wave swarmed in, cramming themselves into every cranny of the suite. Still cameras, video cameras, and cable TV cameras were aimed directly at Donna. She couldn't count how many there were. With lights on and flashing, she couldn't see the photographers, nor could she see the faces behind the notepads and dangling microphones. The windows began to steam up with the contrast of the bright lights indoors and the chilly air outside. At Donna's insistence, Hank and the children stood behind her, although Ben and Nate held their arms over their eyes to avoid the glare.

"Mrs. Brooks, how do you explain these photos?" one reporter started, the microphone practically shoved up Donna's nostril.

"Each of these photos is a lie," she began loud and determined. "They're so absurd that they're funny, except that their intent isn't funny. They are vile misrepresentations that are intended to stir up controversy, damage my good name, cause harm to my loved ones, besmirch my standards and lifestyle, and belittle my product."

Under the lights and the crush of bodies, she startled to work up a sweat, a dew of righteous wrath. But her tone was firm, her cadence controlled and powerful, her emphasis smooth, her pronunciation clear. She felt like she was channeling Elizabeth Cady Stanton. "The paparazzi who are responsible for this *dreck* have taken my life completely out of context and placed it into a wholly unrecognizable form. They have sold their souls. I will not let them sell mine!

"I have never consumed alcohol of any sort. I am fully loyal to my husband. I have never used or abused drugs. At a restaurant, when confronted by flashing cameras, I grabbed the nearest thing to shield my eyes. It happened to be a wine list. At the beach in Massachusetts, a friend and I were started by a noise in the bushes, and I jumped and grabbed onto his arm. My friend thought it was a rodent. It was—of the news photographer variety. Here on the balcony of my room—well, I was prescribed medication for my broken foot. I mean, for heaven sake! Any further explanation about these incidents will be given to my lawyer as we proceed with our plans."

"What plans ..." a reporter asked.

Donna was not to be interrupted. Oh no, she had plenty more to say and plenty to say it to since many of the cameras were on live feed. "For the last few months," she said, "I have been promoting a simple product which is intended to engender some kindness and good will. Throughout this experience, I have found that, time and again, my standards, my lifestyle, and my very identity have been drawn and quartered. I have been told to do this, say that, think this, value that. Attempts have been made to change me into someone I am not. My face, my words, and my every move have been manipulated, massaged, maligned, or lionized depending on the media or the marketer." Where all those m's came from Donna didn't know, but she was moving at too fast a clip to slow down now.

"A human being can sacrifice some privacy and community and security—and can temporarily set aside the comforts of home and family for the promise of a better future. And yes, a human being can be lured away by the siren call of success. I have felt this lure in some small measure, but not, I assure you, in the ways set forth in this ridiculous twaddle.

"I don't navigate these waters smoothly, but I try to be guided first and foremost by an inner rudder and by a power far greater than my own—God's. I am not perfect. But the judgments I make are mine and no one else's—not my family's, not my friends', not my church's. And thanks to the good grace of God, these experiences can be rich fuel for growth for me or anyone else.

"Perhaps by embarking on this voyage, I invited people to judge me. I now realize that I was naive. I have my faults. I chew my nails. I bark at my kids. I am occasionally a klutz, as this broken foot amply demonstrates. I am someone just trying in my own way to do something good and something fun and something that God can be happy about, too. But if I am to be judged, then judge me on the facts, not by these fictions." She dropped the tabloids, letting the pages flutter to the ground.

"Why all this attention on me, anyway? Why can't people use their own considerable energies to do something good and something fun, something that God can be happy about, too—the media, especially, with their considerable talents. This is Christmas, a season of celebration. We should be sharing and singing and being gracious to each other just as God has been to us through the gift of His son. That's my hope for this season—good will toward all men. That's all I have to say."

There was a second of silence and then the reporters surged into a sudden jarring babble. Donna held up both hands and repeated firmly and clearly, "That will be all. Please leave."

It was as if they had been struck mute. The crew began collecting their notes and equipment and then filed out of the suite without saying another word.

"Mother," Stephanie whispered, "to borrow a scriptural phrase, you smote 'em!"

When they were out the door, Hank wrapped his arms around Donna from behind her chair and kissed her, "What a woman!"

Simon was off looking for a can of pop from the mini-bar, but he raised his fist in the air, twirled it around, and whooped a "whoohooo!" Nate and Ben tried to climb up on Donna's lap but her leg was not ready for that.

"Well, that was invigorating!" she said, smiling.

The phone rang. Hank picked up. "It's Margo," he said. He dragged the phone to Donna.

"Girlfriend, you were dynamite!" Margo said.

"Did those photos upset you?" Donna asked. "They were awful!"

"I saw them alright," Margo said. "They're all over the place, just like lice. But don't worry. First of all, anybody who knows you thinks these stories are as crazy as that picture of the eight-legged space alien with Harrison Ford's head. Second, your little sermonette has already become the talk of the town. Everyone's oohing and ahhing about it."

"Really? What did I say?" Donna said. She realized she had no memory of what exactly she had said. She remembered the tone, the pace and the flow, the rush she felt in delivering it. But the words? They completely escaped her.

"I gotta run, honey," Margo said. "Dr. Costelli's coming my way. You were terrific. Makes me proud just to know ya! See you soon!"

Immediately the phone rang again. "Donna *darling!*" It was Gloria. "I knew you could do it! Terrific job! That's my little lioness! You ought to see the feedback Lucy's getting. Ever considered a career in politics? I'm serious, Donna. I could put you in touch with the right people. Hey, with that UN guy already in your pocket ... Oops, gotta run!"

"Turn the phone off, would you, Hank?" Donna said. "Gloria's flattery gave me a headache. And my toes are starting to swell again."

"Time for another pain pill?" Hank offered.

"Let's try ibuprofen," Donna suggested. "Who knows what hidden cameras we have."

"Ben and Nate and I are going down to play video games," Simon said. He had his hand on the doorknob and his brothers in tow.

"Not on your life, misters," Donna said.

"What do ya mean, Mom?" Simon said.

"None of us leaves the room. There are reporters out there, and I'm not sending you out to be swallowed up by them," Donna said.

"But you told them off, Mom!" complained Nate. "See, I'll show you. They're all gone." He opened the door. A sudden flash of cameras stopped him like a deer in headlights. Hank leapt across the room, yanked Nate in, and slammed the door shut. Nate slumped against the door and slid to the floor, his rump hitting the hardwood with a thud. "Cool," he said. "We're still famous."

"Let's all try to get along, guys, because we're going to be together today," Hank said.

"All day, Dad?" Stephanie moaned. "But Matt was going to meet me at the pool table this afternoon."

"Matt? Who's Matt?" Hank asked.

"He's the Orlando boy—that tall, gangly kid," Donna said.

"He's not gangly," Stephanie protested.

"He probably doesn't want to see you anyway, now that Mom's a wino," laughed Simon.

"You cut it out!" said Stephanie, clubbing him with a couch pillow.

"Stop it!" said Donna. In calmer tones, she said: "We'll call downstairs and ask for some videos and board games and see if we can actually do something together for a change."

"Can we watch TV all day?" asked Nate.

"No TV. We're going to be on TV, and I for one don't want to be reminded of any of this," she insisted.

"Can we get a room-service lunch?" Simon asked eagerly.

"Sure," Hank said. "I'll make a few calls, including one for security to come and haul these vermin away from our door."

Donna took a nap for most of the afternoon while Hank and the kids watched *Waking Ned Devine* and *Honey I Shrunk the Kids*. Then all six of them played *Life*, in which Donna obtained four children and landed in the poor house. They played *Monopoly*, where Donna got both Boardwalk and Park Place but spent most of the game in jail with no snake eyes to free her.

Room service dinner was grand. Trout—in December no less!—is what Donna ordered; pasta primavera for Hank; and burger varieties for the kids, heavy on the french fries and ketchup. Chocolate cake all around for dessert.

That night, as they were settling in to watch the *Muppets Christmas Carol*, someone knocked on the door. Hank and Donna looked at each other.

"Who is it?" Hank asked cautiously.

"I'm from the front desk, Mr. Brooks. We just received a fax from a Ms. Gloria Hewitt for Mrs. Brooks and she requests that she receive it immediately." Hank looked back at Donna. She shrugged her approval.

"Slide it under the door, please," Hank said.

"Yes, sir. Thank you." Hank picked up the several pages of paper.

"What is it?" Donna asked. "Another hoax? A threat? A death wish?"

"Wow! Really?" asked Simon.

"I was kidding," Donna said.

"No, it's from Gloria," he said, scanning the papers. "But this looks like good news: 'Donna babe, you grabbed the nation by the jingle bells! Look at these figures! Sales are up phenomenally! Who says scandal doesn't sell? No need to wrangle with the lawyers. Good going, gal! Look at these press clips! Love to my favorite tigress! Sleep tight. Call me when you get back to Rottingham.'"

On the bottom of one page was an elaborate chart Lucy Hobbes had printed up with lines indicating sales at various points of the day. There seemed to be a dip corresponding to the time the tabloids hit the streets, then a sharp increase before Donna's interview. Then a slight dip again, and then a sky-rocket leap and continual ascent beginning with Donna's air time.

"These are terrific reports!" said Hank.

"Look at these headlines!" Donna gasped: "'Moral Center Has Sinnamon Scent.' This one says 'Don't Mess with Mrs. Brooks.' Get this!" She cleared her throat and read from the *Denver Post:*

> Snowbird, Utah—With her family surrounding her and her broken foot in a cast from a skiing accident, Donna Brooks, 43, famed inventor and spokeswoman for Sinnamon, blasted the media Monday morning for what she called 'vile misrepresentations', 'ridiculous twaddle,' and 'dreck.' Alternately vehement and generous, Mrs. Brooks categorically denied the rumors in the weekend tabloids of loose morals and hypocrisy. Mrs. Brooks, a devout Mormon, urged writers and photographers to turn their "considerable talents" to a gracious celebration of the Christmas season. Mrs. Brooks proves to be as potent and commanding as the remarkable essence she developed. Sinnamon, the phenomenally popular scent which threatens to outsell crude oil, continues its 'scentsational' rise in sales after Mrs. Brooks' articulate and straight-from-the-hip holiday message.

"Get this from the *Christian Science Monitor*'s op-ed page," Hank said. "It's by that reporter Annabelle Southport."

"She's a White House correspondent, isn't she?" Donna asked.

"I think so. She's that one with the frizzy gray hair and the wire rims. Look, see? There's her picture in the corner. Okay, let me read this:

> I wish I were Donna Brooks. Strong, clever, committed, and kind—even to the pack of wolves I trot flank-to-jowl with on

144

any given day. I would like to have her confidence, not to mention her new income and her comfortable good looks. What is most impressive about Donna Brooks, however, is her candor. Surely any woman who admits that she barks at her kids and chews her nails can be believed in grander matters. Despite the efforts of those ridiculous tabloids, which hopefully line birdcages at this hour, she remains the genuine article: someone human; someone trying to do her best; someone who will freely admit, to use a line from the old gospel tune, that she's "standin' in the need o' prayer." Aren't we all? Imagine! She teaches us nasty reporters a thing or two and then sends us on our way with a "God Bless Us, Everyone." Even in my wish to be her, Donna Brooks teaches me something. I don't need to be anybody besides me. I don't have to fabricate some image of virtue, power, passion, or perfection. In Washington? In corporate America? Who'd a thunk it? She has performed her own kind of Christmas miracle: she has made *this* crusty old sassbag actually want to "do something good, something fun, and something God can be happy about, too." Stop the presses! *This is news!*

Something fell into place for Donna reading—like bones mending, vertebrae aligning. As articulate as she may have been hours ago in the same room packed to the rafters with reporters, she had no words for what she felt now. Here, curled up under Hank's arm, her leg propped on a pillow on the coffee table, she felt taller, straighter, and healthier than she had in months.

"Simon, you're blocking the TV," Ben whined. "I can't see Miss Piggy."

They turned up the volume and Hank and Donna cuddled up together. With a cozy fire and room-service hot cider and caramel corn, they watched Scrooge change his ways through the intervention of ghosts and friendly monsters.

When she went to sleep that night, Donna was sure she was done with friendly monsters for the season. But she was wrong.

22

The monsters were not waiting for them when they arrived home in Rottingham, although there was a monstrous stack of mail. They entered through the garage because there was so much mail in the entryway that the front door wouldn't open.

"Look at all these Christmas cards!" hollered Ben. He took two greedy armfuls and tossed them in the air.

"Who are these people?" Nate asked, examining a family photo card from Venice, California.

Donna glanced over his shoulder. "Haven't got a clue. See what it says on the back."

"I'll read it," said Simon, snatching it out of his brother's hands. "Merry Christmas from the Ethington Family. It was great meeting you at Nordstrom's in San Francisco. We framed your autograph and have it hanging in our kitchen right over the spice cabinet!"

"Here's another picture one," said Stephanie. "This has a cute couple on the front wearing Santa hats. It says: 'The fertility specialists were wrong! We're due in July! We're thinking of naming her Sinnamon! Thank you so much! Janice and Harry Krauss.'"

The percentages broke down into about 50 percent from total strangers, 20 percent from genuine friends, 15 percent from ward and stake members they didn't really know or from old school classmates from twenty years ago, 10 percent from business contacts for either Donna or Hank, and 5 percent from crackpots with vulgar messages or kooky suggestions for Donna.

These last ones—the ones that weren't obscene—got taped to the refrigerator door for the family's amusement.

Several faxes had come in during their time away. Some were the standard junk faxes to save on Jamaica holidays and so on. But there were two others Donna paid closer attention to.

One of them was from Gloria: "We're making it easy on you these next two days. First: a party at the Museum of Fine Arts in Boston tonight, the 22nd. Rico's worked up a great dark-green velvet number for you with an adorable red muffler to slide up around your cast. He's also got a perky little white apron for you with holly boughs and a couple sprigs for your hair and streamers for the wheelchair. We'll be by tonight at 7:00 to spruce you up. This is nearly the last hurrah. For the grand finale, a state house ball tomorrow night, the 23rd, with the governor. We think Teddy Kennedy will be there. And then, sweetie pie, the fat lady sings! You'll be on your own with our best wishes for a happy and lucrative future. Happy holidays! Gloria."

The other fax was from Sister Monson. It wasn't to Donna directly. It was a copy of a letter she sent to Donna's stake president and bishop:

Dear brethren,

As you have no doubt discovered, Sister Donna Brooks of the Commonwealth Falls First Ward, the inventor and promoter of Sinnamon, has had a significant setback. I have been at her side through the marketing of her product and have encouraged her to promote the best interests of the Church. My vigilance on behalf of the cause of truth, alas, has met with calamity. She has obviously had serious lapses in the area of avoiding the appearance of evil. This is true regardless of the actual circumstances of the photos. Her casual attitude toward the principle in general was apparent from the earliest stages of her rise to worldly fame. I'm sure Sister Brooks is as outraged as much as every faithful saint must be at the negative publicity generated by this sad circumstance. I encourage you, brethren, to be compassionate with Sister Brooks in the judgments which are likely to follow. Please feel free to call upon me if you should need further information.

Yours in the Gospel,
Sister Meredith Monson.

"Who does she think she is?" Hank said, suddenly red in the face. He slammed a cabinet door closed in his hunt for the cocoa mix. "What kind of holier-than-thou woman is she?"

"Let it go, Hank," said Donna calmly. "The cocoa's to the left of the sink."

"You're going to just let her steamroll you into ... some kind of difficulty through these insinuations? It sounds like she's asking them to call a church court on you, doesn't it?"

"That's not going to happen," Donna said. "She's extreme, Hank. She's doing the best she can."

"After all the grief she's put you through, you're going to sit there and tolerate that kind of nonsense?"

"It is odd, isn't it?" Donna mused. "I mean, I don't feel any anger toward her. I don't know what it is, but the outrage is gone. Maybe it was that tirade with the reporters. Maybe I got it off my chest and just don't feel it anymore. I don't think I'm tolerating her, exactly. Yeah, she's pompous and manipulative, but it's just ... silly. It's something to ignore rather than to get all in a huff about. I feel like I've got better things to do than let her mow me down."

"Better things like what?" Hank asked.

"Better things like having hot chocolate with my family, like looking forward to the ward Christmas Carol Sing-In, like really practicing that goodwill to all message I was preaching yesterday."

The holiday parties at the Museum of Fine Arts and the state house were wonderful, festive occasions that were, in fact, a nice way to end the promotional tour. The MFA was festooned with

148

huge pine-bough wreaths with red velvet ribbons. The outfit Rico made matched the setting perfectly—even the red muffler for her cast. It was the same festive ambiance at the state house ball where they served New England clam chowder and corn bread. Ted Kennedy was indeed on hand and took Donna for a spin around the ballroom in her wheelchair. She noticed several photographers taking shots of them. Who would ruin whose reputation? she chuckled to herself. Much to her surprise, Senator Orrin Hatch was also there and took a turn at the piano making up a "Scents of Christmas" ditty as a present for her. She thought it would have made a perfect jingle if she had intended to continue marketing Sinnamon. But she had no such intention.

So it was that on Christmas Eve morning, Donna woke up to find herself formally finished with her career in marketing. There had been some benefits. She really *had* purchased tickets for a trip to Disney World for the day after Christmas. The kids didn't know yet. They would find the tickets in their stockings the next morning. Donna would no longer have to worry about her wardrobe or make-up in the same way, although she had learned a lot from Maddy and Rico and now knew what to look for. She had enough money salted away in market accounts and mutual funds that college tuition and mission funds were looking pretty healthy. That left enough for the new sewing machine she would treat herself to during the after-Christmas sales. She had not become stupid enough to stop shopping for bargains.

After a delicious and cheerful dinner that evening with Margo and her girls, who were home from college, Donna and Hank and the kids headed to the chapel for the Christmas Carol Sing-In. It was an occasion when the bishop winked at the rule about no brass instruments in the chapel. There would be trumpets and tympani, as there were every year. And every year the bishop felt guilty enough about it to print a disclaimer about this not being a regular worship service.

For Donna, it was one of the most worshipful services of the year. There were dignified decorations, the familiar Christmas scriptures read from the gospels, simple music and wonderful solos by some exceptional voices, and tasty, homemade refreshments. There were no sermons. She was up for this! Stephanie and Simon were supposed to hand out programs, so they arrived twenty minutes early.

When Hank came around to help Donna hobble out of the car, Donna noticed Juliet pulling up in her Camry with someone next to her in the front seat. For a moment, Donna couldn't place her. Then she knew. It was Ellen Young! To see her on church property was disorienting.

"Merry Christmas, Donna!" shouted Juliet. She helped Ellen out of the car. "So sorry to hear about your foot—and the rest of your troubles."

"Oh, it's nothing. Merry Christmas to you, too!" Donna said. "And a very merry Christmas to you, Ellen! How wonderful to join us tonight."

"Don't get your hopes up," grumped Ellen. "Just came for the singing."

Juliet winked at Donna. "Oh, I didn't get a chance to tell you. I've got some other visitors coming tonight," she said. "Here they come now. I'm going to take Ellen in. Would you hold back and bring these other folks in with you?"

A white Jeep had pulled into the lot. Out came Lois Wheaton and Ozzie and Franny Lee, Ozzie carrying his trumpet case.

"What a wonderful surprise!" Donna called. "Hank, these are my friends from the Vineyard! Kids, say hi to Lois and the Lees." With hugs and handshakes all around, the happy group made their way into the building.

"Ozzie, are you playing for us tonight?" Donna asked. "What an honor!"

"Juliet put me up to toodling a few Messiah passages. Wynton ain't the only brother can do both jazz and classical, you know what I'm sayin'?"

"This is a treat for us, too, Donna," said Franny. "You have a real home-town kind of feel here, and it's nice to see you and the kids again and to meet Hank. When Juliet told us about this, we couldn't resist!"

"Me, either," added Lois.

"We'll catch up with y'all after the performance, okay? Nate and Ben, you guys think you can lead us to where the musicians are warming up?" Ozzie asked. It wasn't too difficult a task since there was a lot of squawking, tooting, and clanging coming from the Relief Society room.

"No cameras tonight, Lois?" asked Margo. "Does that mean Big Apple's going to miss out on this wonderful photo-op?"

"I think it's had all the photo-ops it needs!" Donna laughed.

"That's for sure," Lois confided. "With the fiasco last week and the way you were sabotaged in the media, I decided to sever my ties with Big Apple."

"That was a real stink, wasn't it?" laughed Margo. "Did you hear our tart-tongued gal tell off those reporters? Isn't she something?" Margo gave Donna a squeeze.

"What do you mean, you're severing your ties with Big Apple?" asked Donna.

"I did a little sleuthing—followed the paper trail of who paid whom for those lurid photos. I felt bad since one was taken right there on my property," she said, her voice hushed a little. "I found out that Gloria Hewitt paid for those."

"Wha-what?" cried Donna. She felt suddenly faint like she might throw up. She leaned heavily into Hank.

"Gloria? The promoter at Big Apple? The one who does all the arranging?" asked Margo.

"Are you sure?" asked Hank.

"I've got it all documented. You can use it if you want, Donna," Lois said. "Yes, it seems Gloria either arranged for the photos or set out her hounds to locate anything they could find that was remotely compromising. She paid a pretty penny for

151

them, too. It was a scheme she had all worked out. It's all in the timing, you know. She timed it perfectly to hit right before Christmas. The biggest bang for her buck.

"Donna, she knew you well enough to know how you'd react to that kind of savage publicity stunt. Of course, you behaved as she expected. To you and me, the way you reacted is a matter of heart and soul. I've become persuaded that Gloria doesn't have a soul. To her, it's just like everything else—a commodity that can be sold for the highest dollar. She didn't care about the impact on you or your family, only what this gamble might do for her profits. It paid off for her. I'm so sorry she put you through this trauma; there is no excuse for that kind of emotional brutality. I just couldn't stay on with them any longer. If I were paid for another project from Big Apple, I'd worry about whose blood money it was."

"I ... I don't know what to say," Donna sighed.

"That heartless witch!" Margo hissed.

"Is that legal? Can she do that?" Hank asked.

Just then Bishop Herlihy tapped the microphone and announced from the pulpit, "Brothers and Sisters, friends and neighbors, we are delighted to welcome you here to our annual Christmas Carol Sing-In ..." Donna hobbled in. She and Hank sat with Nate and Ben in the back row. Margo and Lois sat with Juliet and Ellen Young. Ozzie and Franny Lee were up front, Franny turning the pages for the pianist.

After some reflection, Lois's news didn't seem to be so surprising after all. There were a few tugs of disappointment and stabs of betrayal. Donna found that singing "Angels We Have Heard on High" was especially difficult with its incessant "Glo——rias" in every verse. But the music, the scriptures, the company, the beauty of the evening as it progressed all made Donna feel better. The grim disclosure was more static, more dismal noise to put aside when there was so much more important news to pay attention to at the moment. "Joy to the world, the

Lord is come. Let earth receive her king!" the congregation sang. "Let every heart prepare him room, and Saints and angels sing!"

****

The trip to Disney World was a success and everyone came home tanned and happy. Donna had some adjusting to do two weeks later when her cast came off and one leg was fish-belly white and the other bronzed nearly vixen brown. But for New England winters, long pants were the order of the day anyway.

Every morning as she sent her kids off to school and her husband to work, she was so happy to be in her own comfortable world. Granted, that world included a few new comforts: a new sewing machine, a cell phone, a fax, and the occasional invitation to speak at a school, the local women's club, or a fireside around the stake. She thought she might not tolerate the smell of cinnamon anymore, let alone Sinnamon, but she liked them both as much as she ever did. She was content in nearly every way.

Then one day in February she got a phone call. "Sister Brooks, this is President Redd," said the stake president. "Are you and your husband free to meet with me this evening, say around 8:00 at the stake center?"

Oh no, Donna thought. Sister Monson's fax! I forgot all about it. Is this the first stage of a "court of love?" "Um ... Sure," stammered Donna. "We'll be there."

They arrived at 7:58. Donna clutched Hank's hand in a death grip as they walked into the stake president's office.

"So glad you could make it on such short notice, Sister Brooks, Brother Brooks," President Redd said. "As you know, Sister Meredith Monson has been serving as stake Public Affairs director." Donna felt clammy all over. Her hearing dimmed. Her vision narrowed to the tiny space right in front of her eyes— President Redd's moving lips.

"Sister Monson has been given a new assignment. She will be typing the ward bulletin in her ward. We think it will be a great growth opportunity for her. We have a growth opportunity for you, as well, Sister Brooks. I want to extend to you the calling of ..."